HE BOOK OF
REVELATIONS

A collection of short stories

Daragh Fleming

D1341282

RIVERSONG
BOOKS

An Imprint of Sulis International Press
Los Angeles | London

THE BOOK OF REVELATIONS: A COLLECTION OF SHORT
STORIES BY DARAGH FLEMING
Copyright ©2019 by Daragh Fleming. All rights reserved.

Library of Congress Control Number: 2019905589
ISBN (paperback): 978-1-946849-48-9
ISBN (eBook): 978-1-946849-49-6

Riversong Books
An Imprint of Sulis International
Los Angeles | London

www.sulisinternational.com

Contents

For Catherine, Paul, Cillian, and Dave.

"The race is long, and in the end, it's only with yourself."

-Baz Luhrmann

Preface

I wrote my first short story when I was twelve years old. It was about a leprechaun, and it wasn't very good. Still, I remember my mother telling me that someday I'd have a future in writing. I didn't believe her.

This is the first body of work I've ever created that came from a place of pure desire and ambition. In school and college, I worked hard, but every result came from a place of obligation. It's hard to pour life into something if your heart isn't really in it. This collection, this book, it was born from an itch. It came to be because I felt I had to write these stories down. That's what makes them special for me.

This is The Book of Revelations. I didn't name it that for any religious reasons. It was named because each of these stories reveals something. They try to shine a light on what it means to be human. We struggle, we think, we work, we laugh, we get into the most bizarre circumstances; we live. Each story is different. Some take you off guard, some put you in a situation you'd never think you'd be in. Every single one of them intends to make you think, and if that happens, then I'll consider it a job well done.

I hope you enjoy reading these as much as I enjoyed writing them. They're weird. They're so weird.

Embrace the madness and enjoy the journey.

There's a Lack of Youth in Asia

The human body demands sleep. It necessitates it. We spend about a third of our lives asleep on average, some more, some less. I read once that scientists can't even figure out why we need to sleep. It has something to do with a defect in cells that cause them to exhaust. I don't know the whole story with all of that really, too brainy for me to be honest. What I do know is that, although most nights I sleep fine, and it's normal and easy, sometimes I'm afraid to go to sleep. I'm not sure if that's weird or not, but it feels like it will be. It's one of those things you can't gauge for weirdness because you've never heard anyone ever have that same experience. It's like saying you're afraid of being a lemon. How could you know for sure if that was a common fear? You couldn't, and you'd be reluctant to disclose your fear in case it was too weird. That's what it feels like for me to be afraid to go to sleep sometimes. I don't know if that's an okay thing for me to be fearful of, or whether it's just childish.

When I was younger, there was this noise that used to scare me. It was like a really light clicking that used to move around the room and it came at various volumes. Sometimes it was far away and quiet, sometimes it was right next to my ear and loud. It used to keep me up all night, terrified. I remember it would go quiet, and just as I was falling asleep, the noise would be right here, next to my ear and very intrusive. I'm not saying the sound was alive, but it felt like it. Now, the noise still follows me, I'm just not afraid of it anymore. What's even weirder is that it isn't only in my room at home. It follows me everywhere I sleep, whether that be in a different room in the same house, or a different country entirely. I'm a bit sceptical to say that I'm haunted by a noise, but the evidence is there. I read online that it was some sort of tiny bug that makes the noise. But I've never seen a bug in my room like that, and I doubt any bug would have the conscious capacity to follow around one specific individual just to scare him at night time in a variety of locations.

To be honest, the noise is just a bit of background information. It's not the reason that I'm afraid to go to sleep, sometimes. The real reason I'm afraid to nod off is because of these small panic attacks I get. They're not overwhelming and exhausting like full-blown panic attacks, but they do enough to scare me into being fully awake. I panic and can't focus on anything else, and I'm just consumed by thoughts of this one thing. The reason I'm afraid to sleep sometimes is that I can't stop imagining what it would be like to be dead. Specifically, I imagine what it's like to lack consciousness, to feel, or know nothing. To cease existing. It's very uncomfortable, and it relates so much to how sleeping feels that it scares me from wanting to do that. There is something very unsettling, but at the same time very natural, about not existing. See, it's something that happens to all of us eventually, yet we know very little about it. We don't exist for a far longer time than we ever exist, in this way, in this body. Maybe we do reincarnate, but if we can't remember the past life we led, then you may as well be a brand new person, anyway. I think dead people have secrets.

The idea of death scares me so much that I don't want to sleep. This makes for some very productive nights, as usually, I can sense the fear coming on and know that sleep will elude me. I try to do something productive on these nights; work-out, plan my week, do bits of work here and there. That motivation dwindled over time. It's a redundant process. Thinking of death, even though it scares me, is addictive. I almost want to think about it, I want to be afraid. It's like when you smell a bad smell. You hate the smell, but somewhere inside you, you still have the urge to go ahead and take another whiff. If I'm candid with you, and I may as well be, the thing that scares me the most isn't the thought of death, it's the fact that the notion of death entices me. Death is something I look forward to, and there's a large part of me that is terrified by this sinister desire. It's as if part of me is corrupted and is a source of anguish for the rest of me on these nights when I am consumed by death. I'm so scared of this other part of me, this 'death-lover', that I'm afraid to go to sleep in case that part somehow figures out how to keep us there, to keep us dead.

Sometimes this other part of me is stronger than me, and it takes over. It consumes our brain with thoughts of death. It's a cold darkness. He makes us want to move towards our demise. Sometimes he's so strong that, he can take over our brain during the day, even when I'm with my few friends and family. Although I still control my body, he's very talented at manipulating me into thinking his glorious death is a desirable option. He contorts our mind and shrouds my better judgement with doubt. Some days he's stronger than others, and there are times when I don't feel his presence for weeks at a time. But he always comes back in the night, making death attractive, and scaring me into staying awake. He taunts and tempts and promises that we're better off dead, and sometimes I believe him.

He often comes with a variety of quick, painless ways to kill us, in some distorted attempt to ease me into the idea. Lately, I've felt weak against his attacks, and that's when I start to listen. This other part of me, the one obsessed with being dead, he isn't a monster. He's not evil. He just has a very, very different idea of what will bring him/us happiness. To him, I guess I'm the one trying to stop his happiness. There's a lot of stigma that surrounds dying by your own hand though. Not that it would make a difference to me in the grand scheme of it all, but I'm sure that there would still be a deep, Catholic shame in my family. See, to be honest, I've been dead for years, in a virtual sense. Some people die early in life but continue to live, and I think that maybe I'm one of these people. I don't have an explanation for this. There was no cataclysmic event, no terrible trauma that forced me to become this way, it merely happened. I've been dead for years. I have no preference for death or life. The other part of me, however, has a clear preference for death, and since it doesn't affect me either way too strongly, I've been considering letting him have this one and final win.

I've thought of my family and friends already, and how this could affect them. I'm more concerned about my friends, really. We live in a society that shames self-annihilation, and I'll be painted as a monster, even though this isn't really my choice. My family will survive. As I said there is a deep-rooted Catholic tradition in my extended family, and there's a chance that they'll disassociate from me now that I'm 'one of those'. Over the last few years, my family have all but abandoned me, anyway. They have their own lives, and I get that. Still, I've had to grow used to being alone. I've had to take care of myself for the most part. I don't think they left me alone on purpose, they just prioritize their own lives over me. I've recently begun to feel like a burden. Maybe they'll act as if I never existed once the funeral is over. It doesn't bother me really, I won't be around to experience it.

I'm just tired. I'm so, so tired. For these last few years, I've had these moments of weakness where I'm afraid to fall asleep. I've been afraid of death. I've been afraid of the part of me that silently wishes for death. But now, I'm so tired that I'm not really afraid. I see death as a release, as the next chapter in my existence. I'm tired of just existing, and I've had enough loneliness in the last few years to last two life-times. Some people may argue with this, but that's fine too. I've talked to my doctors about it already. All I have to do is sign some insurance form, and the next time I go to sleep, I simply won't wake up. It was tough leaving home to come here, but euthanasia is illegal where I'm from. Tonight, however, I won't be afraid to sleep. Tonight I'll finally get some rest. At 92 years old, I'm exhausted by life, and I reserve the right to die when I want.

46A-pathy

Have you ever heard of the bystander effect? It's this old so-cial psychology phenomenon that says if there is an event that requires urgent attention, you as an individual will be less likely to act if there are other people present. It means that you'll assume someone else will sort out the problem, instead of taking the lead yourself. You've experienced this before, everyone has. It's the reason they make those ads about smelling as in the street. I haven't stopped thinking about this effect since I fully experienced the repercussions of it.

I'd just finished a shift at work. I worked in a high-end retail store on O'Connell Street bang in the middle of Dublin. It was the closing shift which means you're the last to go home. In Dub-land that can be a good thing though because it means you beat the initial panicky, anxious 5pm rush home. It was 8 o'clock now, and there wasn't as palpable an atmosphere of urgency. From where I left the shop, there was a stop for the 46A right across the road. I never got the bus there. If I did, it would mean paying the higher price of €2.65, whereas if I walked 400 metres down the road, and across O'Connell's Bridge to get the same bus, it would only cost €2.05. Now you might think 60 cent isn't much, but it is when you're a student and need to buy naggins at the weekend. Pints in Dublin are outrageously priced as well. Anyway, I locked the door behind me, zipped up my cheap parka jacket in an attempt to keep out the cold, and started walking.

The orange text of a Dublin Bus sign is hard to make out from far away, even if your vision is perfect. I always figured that they did this on purpose, in an attempt to make you come closer to see what was really going on. It would be a pure Fianna Fáil thing to do. I could get two buses home from here, the 46A or the 145, both worked. The 46A would arrive first in two minutes, according to the live schedule above my head, so I decided I'd take that one. The 145 was usually quicker, but I didn't want to be out in the cold for longer than I needed to be. The usual hampering of tired commuters huddled around the bus-stop. Most had their headphones in to keep human-interaction at a minimum. I was no different. There were a handful of elderly people around. I quietly placed wagers on which one would be the entitled go-getter that felt they had a right to get on the bus first, just because they had been living longer than the rest of us. I chose a small, white-haired woman, standing as close to the stop as possible, feverishly scrunching an old napkin in her hands. Her head was tilted slightly upwards so that, even if she were talking to a person taller than her, it would appear that she was looking down at them while speaking. Her nose was angled ever so slightly upwards, ensuring she'd have to gaze down the barrel of her nose to make eye contact with anyone. As the bus stop grew busier, and she was nudged by the odd passer-by, you could see her kissing her teeth, holding back an outburst of privileged fury. 'Oh yes,' I thought. 'This is the one.'

Soon after my selection, the 46A's headlights appeared on O'Connell's Bridge, the bulk of its body lurching silently forwards. As per usual, the bus stopped 20 metres too long, and its prospective customers fumbled awkwardly toward it, agitated by the slight inconvenience. I had utterly wronged the old one who waited nervously for her turn to board the bus. I was feeling bad for my quick judgment, when a battle-ax came barging past from out of sight, willing her way to the top of the queue. 'Ahh', I thought, 'There's my girl'. I smirked to myself as the self-righteous middle-aged woman successfully pushed her way into the bus. People can be ignorant at the best of times.

As I boarded the bus, I paid my well-earned lower fare of €2.05. The peeling laminate of my leap card scraped off of the metal of the metre, as the faint beep confirmed my payment. I shuffled along and up the stairs to the top deck of the bus. I generally have shit balance so the usual stumble and stagger, followed by unnecessary apologies, were brought about by the jerky movement of the bus as it took off again. I always sit on the top deck of the bus. This isn't so I can look out the windows. The bright lights of the buses interior make it challenging to see out the windows at night, anyway. I usually sit on the top so I can watch people. Often, it's the weird people, the risk-takers that sit up top. You wouldn't catch the old woman with the white hair up here, too highly strung. You certainly wouldn't find anyone from the upper-classes there either, not with the petty-common folk. The top deck of a Dublin Bus can be compared to flying with Ryan-Air. There's no shame in it, but some people are just too good for that lark. I made my way to an empty two-seater about a third of the way down the bus and collapsed into the inside seat. Sometimes I'd sit on the outside and put my backpack on the inside seat so that I don't have to endure unwanted companionship disturbing my journey home. That day though, I didn't feel like being a prick, and the bus was fairly busy, so I didn't want to risk the awkwardness of someone asking me to push in. That'd be the worst.

The bus pulled out and edged forward. Traffic was heavy and as I mentioned the bus was fairly busy. I quietly celebrated that nobody had sat next to me yet. A small victory after a long day. The bus stopped three or four times in quick succession. People coming and going from our top-deck, like bees from a hive.

I noticed him before he saw me. My awareness of him was more than likely the reason he chose to sit next to me. The Law of Attraction was a cruel bitch. Everyone else purposely avoided his gaze or genuinely hadn't seen him. For all intents and purposes, this man was a tramp. He wore ripped tracksuit bottoms, which were one of those knock-off brands you'd find in Penney's or Dunnes. He had a plain navy hoodie on with a light, black raincoat over it. Pure clashing. He was overweight, with short, dirty brown hair and teeth like the ones your mother warned you about if you ate too many sweets. I got the feeling this tooth decay didn't come from sweets though. He had a can of Gallahad in his right hand, a struggling, plastic bag from Lidl in his left. The movement of the bus made him stumble and trip down the aisle, ignorantly spilling beer on disgusted copassengers. He eventually reached my row, and my body instinctively tensed up as his scent reached my nostrils, burning into my brain. He grunted suggestively in my direction as he sat down. I assumed this was his way of asking if he could sit, so I nodded in response. He smelled the way curtains smell in a damp abandoned house, mixed in with stale alcohol and unwashed skin. His face was poorly shaved, so the hair was all patchy and dirty. I kept my headphones in, knowing an interaction was inevitable and imminent.

A few minutes passed. I could see him looking at me. I could feel his dry eyes bearing into me. I could smell the stale alcohol on his breath. He grunted at me. I pretended I didn't hear him with my headphones in. He grunted again, this time louder and more purposeful. He turned into me as he did so that I'd know he was gesturing at me. I took the earphone out of my right ear and looked toward him. He grunted at me and gestured at his can of Gallahad and then to this bag. Initially, I was confused but soon realised he was offering me a can. I smiled uncomfortably and declined, putting my earphone back in. As much as I liked cans, drinking with a tramp on a public bus wasn't exactly my scene.

"Where yer goin?'" he slurred at me, spitting as he did so. I only just about caught the end of the sentence and paused as I figured out what he wanted.

"Oh…eh, Stillorgan," I answered vaguely. I didn't live there, but it was close enough that it would satisfy the question. He perked up at the sound of Stillorgan and smiled, showing his yellow-brown teeth.

"Stillorgan! Me too," he smirked back. It may have been my prejudice, but I was reasonably confident that this man only said he was going to Stillorgan because I was going there. In fact, the way he said it, it almost felt as if he was implying that he would be joining me for the remainder of the evening. I felt pretty uncomfortable. Another few stops came and went. Out of the corner of my eye, I could see the tramp rummaging around in his plastic bag. I tried to ignore this and kept my gaze looking directly forward, out of the front of the bus, looking down on Leeson Street. I felt the tramp nudge me with his elbow and looked down. The fella was holding an unpackaged, unsliced, 18-inch loaf of stale bread. He held it towards me, signalling that I should take it. I looked around. People were beginning to stare at what was going on. Was this some sort of payment for allowing the man to accompany me to Stillorgan? I wasn't even really going there. What was his game plan with this loaf of bread? Who was it originally intended for? Surely he hadn't bought this loaf intending to use it as barter. Maybe he had. Either way, I began to shake my head urgently in rejection of his offer. His eyes looked defeated as he reluctantly stowed the 18-inch loaf back inside his Lidl bag. I let out a quiet sigh of relief. I could feel the humiliation radiating off of him.

11 WITHDRAWN

A few swigs of his second can of Gallahad since boarding the bus relieved me of some of the guilt I was feeling. He was clearly moving on. As we neared the stop, directly across the N11 from the main entrance to UCD, he started to stir, readying his tattered Lidl bag to disembark the busy bus. As he rose from his seat, he immediately started stumbling forward; the effects of the alcohol combined with the jerky movements of the bus making it difficult to stand upright. He let out an irritated grunt as he regained his balance and slowly lurched forward, step-by-step. His journey to the stairs was tedious and wavering, which gained indirect taunts from other passengers, mocking the inebriated state of the homeless man struggling to walk forward.

The bus was still moving when he reached the top of the stairs. He wore a proud smirk on his face, satisfied with the progress he had made. As the tramp took his first descending step, the bus driver suddenly slammed on the breaks. This was too much for the drunk man's unsteady legs. His almost-empty can immediately leaped into the air as his legs gave out from underneath him. The man yelped as he fell headfirst down the stairs. This was met with a chorus of laughter from the top deck which reverberated around the bottom deck as passengers realised what had happened. As the tramp crashed down the stairs, he nicked his neck on one of the cylindrical bins that are meant for bus tickets, which nobody really uses. The cut wasn't too bad, but it began bleeding immediately. The alcohol in his system had thinned his blood, making the small wound look worse than it was.

The laughing died down as the homeless man staggered off of the bus, the events that had just taken place had sobered him up. From my seat, I peered down at him. His face was shadowed over by the streetlight above, but I could see by the faint glint that his eyes were gazing up at me. His left hand was now held over the gash on his neck and blood was beginning to soak into his hoodie, making the navy grow darker. He looked disheartened and confused as the bus pulled away again.

I had laughed along with everyone else. It was impulsive. It was socially normal, almost expected of me. As the bus pulled into my stop by the Radisson, I questioned whether I'd have laughed if that man wasn't homeless. As I walked through the darkened forest path to my house I wondered if a 'regular' person had fallen, would anyone have laughed? If the man wasn't drunk, would someone have gotten up to help him stand? If he didn't smell the way he did, would someone have made sure an ambulance was called so that his neck would stop bleeding? Undoubtedly so. I turned the key in my door and walked into a dark, deserted house. All the lads were asleep I figured. The homeless man, and how we had treated him, still played on my mind. We had treated him as less than. Him being homeless meant that, he was supposed to be drunk and that it didn't matter where he ended up or what had happened to him. Guilt burned my ears red as I thought about how he had tried to befriend me, and how I had dismissed him. I fell asleep that night wondering if, had I fallen down the stairs, would I have been left to wander off into the cold, Dublin evening?

I woke the next morning to the default ringtone of the iPhone alarm, 7:30am. Like every other morning, I started my day by flicking through my Twitter feed. Plenty of memes, something about Conor McGregor doing something stupid, again, and then a thread of tweets from some radio show's News updates caught my eye. Near the Tesco in Merrion, an unnamed man was found dead in the early hours of the morning, having bled out from a neck wound in the cold. He appeared to be homeless. My face went numb, and I could feel the blood draining from it. The cut on his neck must have been worse than it seemed. After all, nobody had bothered to check on the man from the bus. The combined ignorance of the passengers of the 46A had led to the death of a helpless, homeless man. The guilt which had just come to fruition was soon amplified by a dawning realization;

What if every homeless death is caused by our collective ignorance?

An Origin in Celery

Doctor Barton Miller scurried through the dimly lit hallways of Lab 27. He wasn't meant to be there; nobody was at this time of night. Barton was in a rush. He needed to extract his most prominent research and destroy the rest. His glasses slid down his hurried along the corridor. He could have done this commute with his eyes closed. This place had been his Mecca for the last 17 years. Doctor Miller developed some of the most influential genetic research of the last century here; things that would change and save the world. But now it had become corrupted. The higher-ups, the suits that were never seen, only their will heard, had shown their full hand. They weren't going to use his research as he'd intended; they were going to militarize it. Genetic warfare, a new era of terror in the world, based solely off of genetically modified plant material. In terms of saving the world, it simply meant being able to grow crops in virtually any environment. However, if the research was applied to the human genome with the right funding, it meant the age of super-soldiers was imminent. Miller's conscience couldn't let him live in a world where his research was the cause of so much destruction, and so as soon as word had reached his department of the new direction for the company, he had decided that his research must be sabotaged, and any evidence of it removed from the archives.

Barton slid through the door of the lab as he had done countless times before and flicked the switch on the wall to his left without looking. This initiated a low hum, followed by the blinking of one of the overhead lights. The ceramic white of the countertops reflected the light, causing the room to glow brilliantly. The room appeared how Barton imagined Heaven would be; perfectly clean and in order. He'd planned this escapade for weeks and knew it would take under 4 minutes to complete. His most prominent, and therefore most dangerous research, had been regarding the genetic splicing of a very resilient and efficient strain of bacteria found only in the craters of active volcanoes around the Pacific Rim. Miller had figured out how to extract the DNA strands which allow for this resilience and merge it with the DNA of staple and everyday vegetables. In short, Miller had produced vegetables such as potatoes, carrots, celery and broccoli which can thrive in the harshest and most depleted environments. The research, if it were to be made mainstream, was effectively a cure for world hunger, as virtually all crops would be capable of growing anywhere on the planet.

As the fluorescent lights withdrew the lab from darkness, the terribly corporate company logo glared back at Barton from each of the four walls. The company, trading as Omnitech Industries, had recently picked up a military contract which, in return for a deliciously large funding grant, resulted in any past and current projects to be under the ownership of the federal government and its military. This meant that the military could pick and choose whichever projects they sought and use them at their own discretion to advance any agenda they might have. There were hundreds of potentially catastrophic possibilities, considering how cutting-edge the facilities and projects were at Omnitech. Barton Miller led a team that focused solely on all things biological or biomaterial, outside of the animal kingdom. Under his supervision, there had been countless investigations into bio-hazardous gases, liquids, and other substances, all of which could be weaponised and used in chemical warfare.

On top of that, Barton's precious bacteria-resilience project had the possibility to be applied to humans, which was an unexplored, and frankly irresponsible direction in which to take his work. Barton's work could, in theory, make humans resilient to 99% of all ailments, diseases, and illnesses, which would effectively make mankind immortal. Barton knew that if word of this got out, it would be acted upon, without considering the repercussions of having an immortal parasite dominate the Earth. He also felt that this came far too near to 'playing God' and although Barton wasn't religious, he still didn't want to take the chance.

He whisked around the room with sublime precision. He flicked off the genetic splicer and grabbed the vials which has been spinning in its main compartment. He took a strong electro-magnet from his backpack and began meticulously holding it to each of the 3 hard drives and 4 back-up hard-drives which held all his team's research. He had already backed-up the most promising and up-to-date research onto a personal hard-drive which was stored in a secret underground safe at his family's estate. He knew he could never return to work here. It was too risky, especially when there would be a comprehensive investigation into how all the research had been destroyed. It could all be replicated eventually, but it would take years. Barton understood that they'd soon know it was he who destroyed the lab. Not returning to work would be a massive indicator that he was the culprit. It was just too risky to hide in plain sight, subtlety wasn't Miller's forte. He'd spend the rest of his life looking over his shoulder, on the run. Still, it was a fair price to pay for the safety of the world, and the preservation of his own conscience.

Before leaving, Barton had to collect the viable crops that had been generated from the genetically modified seeds he had developed. They had been stored in a vacuum-sealed room near the back of the lab. Out of the batch, only four had survived. Other trials had resulted in a severe mutation of the plants. One trial had caused a grotesque rash to spread across the entirety of one of the technician's torsos after he made direct skin contact with a Golden Wonder Potato. He had been kept in isolation for 4 months before they figured out how to reverse the effects.

The crops had been planted in 4 separate, mobile containers. There was a potato plant as mentioned, along with cucumber, celery, and cabbage. Although Barton was sure they had gotten rid of the genetic bugs that caused the rash, he still put on a pair of latex gloves before handling the plants. He placed each of the plants into the duffle bag he had stowed in his backpack and closed it shut. The last thing Barton had to do before leaving was wipe the CCTV footage which was easily accessible from the computer at his own desk. Barton scrolled to the file labelled '09/06/22' and promptly deleted it from the desktop. He then quietly left the facilities at Omnitech Industries as unnoticeable as he had entered them. Never planning to set foot in the lab again, Barton began to look ahead to his life on the run.

Cain Randle, the board director of Omnitech, scratched his stubbled-chin and looked down at the footage again. As intelligent as Miller was, he clearly didn't understand the mechanics of deleting digital video. Randle watched the flustered geneticist flurry around the lab, taking what seemed to be random samples and corrupting data drives. He couldn't help the fits of laughter that escaped his usually stoic face. This had been his 16th replay of the footage, and it only got more entertaining. Barton Miller had been a problem alright, but not for the reasons he thought. For years his team had been haemorrhaging money on completely insignificant research. Miller was also completely deluded into thinking his research was in some way a 'game-changer'. The footage was clear evidence of that. Fair enough, their new stakeholders were after some research that Omnitech had been working on, but none of it was anything that had been under Miller's guidance. The board had been waiting for a reason to impose redundancy on Miller, but now they didn't need one. The man's paranoia had become so severe that he had chosen to dispose of himself, which meant no redundancy package, which meant money saved. Miller was deluded, Randle was entertained, the board was satisfied; everybody was a winner.

Barton had been flicking through the news channels all day. There had been no reporting of the break-in he had orchestrated at Omnitech. Maybe he had been so efficient that it went unnoticed? Doubtful. Barton's gut told him that the board was trying to keep the break-in under-wraps, as it would affect the military contract they'd just landed if they had a PR meltdown right now. Barton's concentration was interrupted by the stingy scent of Frank's hot sauce which reached his nostrils from the kitchen. By the smell of things, the chicken wings were almost ready. Barton had spent the last month pre-emptively emptying out the contents of the freezer as he knew he wouldn't be living in his apartment much longer. It had been two days since the break-in, and it was only a matter of time before the wrong people came knocking. This would be his last meal before he went off the grid. He shifted into the kitchen and opened the oven, the invisible wave of chicken-heat hit his face, and the lenses of his glasses fogged up briefly. As he began to prepare his plate for dinner, he heard the newscaster on Channel 4 News mention "Omnitech Industries" and his ears perked up. He grabbed the remote and turned up the television. Barton continued to prepare his meal thoughtlessly as his eyes were fixed on the TV screen on the other side of the open-plan. He watched grainy footage of himself roping around a small laboratory, wasting hard-drives and collecting vials. He piled his plate with wings, washed two sticks of celery and landed himself on the armchair in front of the screen. It didn't take him long to realize that this wasn't so much a Breaking News story as it was a light-hearted fluff news piece. They were laughing at him. The feed switched to a very amused Cain Randle explaining how none of the research stolen was of any value, and that the perpetrator involved (who remained unnamed) had clearly gotten the wrong lab, or was indeed misinformed. The broadcast ended shortly after, as Randle couldn't hold himself together. Barton sat back in his chair. Although he was alone, he could feel the crimson mixture of embarrassment, shame, and fury filling his cheeks. He passive-aggressively took a loud crunch of celery into his mount and chewed it down.

A wave of horrible realization rose from his stomach as the chewed celery was swallowed in the opposite direction. This was no ordinary celery. This was the genetic hybrid celery. This was the genetic hybrid celery that had never been tested for human consumption. Barton must have taken the wrong celery from the fridge. Barton's knees became jelly at the realization of what he'd just eaten. His mind flashed to the horrible rash that had spread all over the lab technician's body, and he began to tremble with fear. The sudden mention of the break-in had stolen his focus from his meal prep. Barton Miller had potentially just swallowed a very fatal mouthful of (admittedly quite fresh) celery.

The effects of the mutant-celery began with vomiting. Violent, vicious vomiting. For two hours Barton wretched up the contents of his insides, which after 30 minutes consisted of nothing but bile and blood. His eyes teared from the painful hammering his chest took from empty retching, and he was sure he wouldn't last the night. As the puking let up, his body was overcome with a fever, paired with harsh body aches. Barton would have assumed it was food poisoning from the chicken, except for the fact that he hadn't even taken a bite from a wing, only a measly mouthful of celery. The mutated genetic mix-up of the celery was taking hold of his body, and he could have no idea of what to expect. That night, he eventually passed out on his armchair, thinking about the technician from the lab who got that rash from one of the first trials of vegetables, and he was certain that he wouldn't get off so lightly.

If you've ever woken up and not known where or who you were for the first moments of wakefulness, you'll understand fractionally how Barton Miller felt when he woke up the next morning. As soon as he had regained consciousness, he knew something was deeply wrong in a way that couldn't be pinpointed. Everything felt off. He couldn't move, nor feel any of his limbs. He considered momentarily that he had entered sleep-paralysis, but even his face felt as though it wasn't there. He could still see, but he was flat on his back, and only the living-room ceiling was in view, which looked bigger than it usually did somehow as if he was further away from it. As his state of paralysis continued to persist, panic began to set in, and Barton used every ounce of will to move his limbs. As he explored his movement, he found that he could move his back marginally, in the same way a turtle can roll on its shell when it finds itself over-turned. Barton began to exhaust all his energy and tried to get himself to roll over. He shifted from left to right, over and over, trying to get some momentum in his swing. He moved his weight from one side to the other to try to kick-start a rolling motion. He'd have been sweating if he were able to, but for some reason, over-heating wasn't an issue right now.

Just as Barton got enough momentum to get momentarily onto his side before falling back onto his back, he stopped rocking. He'd seen something that made him question his entire being, his entire belief system. Barton was lying next to a large, but authentic, chicken wing. In fact, he was surrounded by giant chicken wings, all smothered in Frank's

Hot Sauce, the very same lathering he'd applied to the wings he'd prepared the night before. However, he couldn't smell the wings as his sense of smell was non-existent. The giant wings were indeed disturbing, but they weren't the most harrowing thing Barton had seen as he rolled. As Barton rolled, he'd caught the reflection in a very, very large spoon on the other side of the chicken wing. There was no recognizable reflection of his puffy, spectacled face looking back at him, however. Instead, he saw the reflection of a plate full of chicken wings, and one slender piece of celery, momentarily on its side. It was confusing, it defied all current laws of physics and sense, but he knew it had to be true; Barton Miller had somehow become a piece of raw celery.

Barton lay there for two days trying to figure out how the f**k he'd become a piece of celery. Like all pieces of celery, being out in the open caused Barton to start rotting, which felt a bit like dying from dehydration. The possibility that Barton was dreaming has collapsed as soon as he began to feel the intense pain of rotting in the open. The air around him felt like it was trying to squeeze him to death, pressing down on him from all angles.

Whether he had lost his mind or whether this was really happening, Barton knew he had a limited time frame. As he lay there, considering the existential consequences of him turning into a piece of celery, he noticed something within his mind he hadn't noticed before. There was a switch, just like a light switch, only mental rather than physical. He could feel it, the same way he could feel his ability to speak English. It was a part of his brain. Considering he had no other options, Barton flicked this mental switch. Instantly, there was a loud crack as the plate he lay on split from his exponentially growing weight. He felt his arms descend from his shoulders, his hairbrush his forehead, and his lungs suck in air. Barton now lay on the coffee table in his living room, stark naked on top of a broken plate, with chicken wings and Frank's hot sauce everywhere. Barton was once again a man, and no longer a piece of celery. He could still feel the mental switch in his mind. Soon he would realize that the genetically altered celery he'd mistakenly eaten had given him the ability to transform into a piece of celery, along with some other abilities. Using the same mental switch that was now ever-present in his mind, Barton would learn that he could change from man to celery quite literally at the flick of a switch. It wouldn't be long before Barton would find the courage to test and explore his new powers. He would also have to face the decision of using his newfound powers for good, or for evil. On that day, Barton Miller's life changed forever.

On that day, Barton Miller became Celery Man.

4-Minute Phone Repair

The scent of fresh vomit singed her nostrils. Sam was on all fours, head held cautiously over the rim of the egg-white toilet. She had just dispelled her first bout of vomit in her adult life. It had come out of both her mouth and nostrils. Tears streamed down her face, marking the conclusion of this session of purging. More would come later, much more. Her chest was sore from the pain that empty retching inflicts, the same way it hurts when a burp gets stuck in your esophagus, causing a miniature explosion of gas in the middle of your chest. An endurable pain, but extremely uncomfortable. She looked down at the contents of the toilet, fresh bile dripping from the tip of her button nose. Amongst the unrecognizable gush of lumpy vomit, there were three perfectly formed, somehow unchewed sausages, along with a perfectly preserved piece of bacon. Sam thought she was seeing things from the nausea and dehydration. She wasn't. The breakfast she had had that morning, the breakfast she had definitely chewed up and swallowed, now sat floating, uneaten in the toilet of the SuperMacs on Junction 14 just off the motorway. Had she not just thrown up into an empty toilet, she would have guessed they had been there before she got there. But no. Sam had just thrown up full sausages. Her body had somehow put them back together. She made

25

a mental note to follow this up the next day. Right now, she was extraordinarily hungover and needed to get home.

Sam got sick another 4 times that day. Each time she gawked, she threw up whole-foods. Things she had definitely chewed down had come back up as if nobody had even attempted to digest them. She threw up a full burger, which was followed by the buns. She'd eaten about 8 marshmallows, all of which came out of her, fluffy and perfect. It was only after she threw up a full Cornetto (mint flavour) that she really started to worry about what was going on inside her. She made an urgent appointment with her GP for the next day, explaining that she had a strange vomiting bug. Once she was off the phone, Sam vomited again, which resulted in a full chicken breast and two sticks of celery being dispelled into her toilet.

Naturally, her doctor was stumped. After displaying her new ability to produce perfect preservations of things she'd eaten (A full bagel, which was someone unsliced now), her GP had sxent her straight to a specialized gastroenterologist at the hospital. Sam spent the next two days being tested, eating various foods and being forced to vomit them back up to document the effects her digestive tract had on the foods. Each time she threw up, fully undigested foods were dispelled, and each time it felt as though they were further away from figuring it out. After the two days of relentless testing without any answers, the doctors eventually called in the world's leading expert in biological mutations, Barton Miller. Flying him in from the States was costly, but Sam's condition was a world's first, and it would no doubt have repercussions for the entire planet. Sam's ability was a potential step forward in evolution. Miller was obsessed to the point of lunacy, some would say, with accelerating the evolution of humanity. He had a penchant for making use of any natural mutation, to serve the world and the future of the human race.

The communication between Miller's team of doctors and Sam was on a need to know basis. They compartmentalised everything. She wasn't told much, and she was heavily sedated for the most part. However, on her 6th morning waking in the high-security ward of the European branch of Omnitech's research facilities (which she'd been transferred to on Day 3), there was something very different. Sam woke up alone in the sterile room she was being stored in. It was a stereotype of the type of room you'd expect shady experiments to take place in. Completely, white, with various pieces of equipment tucked away. Her mind was foggy, like she was hungover but without the taste of 3 a.m. tequila in her mouth. Her neck and lower abdomen were tender and painful. It wasn't the type of pain you get from sleeping awkwardly. It was an aching pain, like the pain you get from bruises or cuts. It was medical pain. Sam glanced down and saw the bandages around her torso, which caused her heart to jump into her mouth and her stomach to drop as if she were going over a small hill on a road really quickly. A machine nearby began to beep more rapidly. They had operated on her. They'd cut into her without her consent, and they'd done something to her. She was terrified. She had no idea what they could have done to her. Sam began to panic, and she reached to get out of bed but found that her hands and feet were bound up by chains to the metal frame of the bed. She struggled until exhaustion (which didn't take long as she was still quite heavily sedated). Suddenly a door whizzed open in the corner of the room. A man of average height walked into the room. He was overweight, but still quite handsome. His spectacles complimented the bone structure of his face, and the lines on his cheeks indicated that the man laughed, or at least smiled, quite a lot. Dr. Barton Miller approached Sam's bed timidly. He was obviously quite aware of the ethical implications of operating on a person without their consent. Nonetheless, this wasn't his first time doing so, and he'd gotten quite good at explaining the manner of his research, and why what had just taken place, had to have taken place.

Barton began with a simple summary of human evolution, and how humans hadn't evolved since the Stone Age (which was quite patronising). He explained how, statistically, the species was due an evolutionary leap and that cases such as Sam's had been popping up all over the globe for the last decade. Barton envisaged this leap forward would need to be facilitated by tech-biology bonding of some sort, and so it was under his jurisdiction to guide each new 'specimen' (as he referred to Sam) through their evolving state. He described in unnecessary detail to Sam, quite a lot of the genetic changes that she'd undergone in such a short amount of time, much of which she didn't understand. All the surgery had done was allowed her to use her new body more intuitively, the same way trousers are designed to allow full function of the legs, whilst making the rest of the body more comfortable in the process.

Sam could consume any broken material and vomit it back up reconstructed as if it had never been broken. The surgery had simply made this process more streamline. Miller's team had installed a sort-of-button on Sam's neck. It was essentially a thicker-than-usual inverse-condom connecting to the inside of her throat. The button's purpose was to make it easy and efficient for Sam to reach the back of her throat and induce the body's gag reflex so that she could throw up on command. The rubber inverse condom extended inwards to her throat so Sam could easily, and quite hygienically cause herself to vomit. After several uses of the term 'inverse-condom', Sam requested that they retire this name for the new button on her neck.

The second upgrade was a flexible docking station which entered Sam's stomach from the outside, near the left oblique. The station looked similar to a resealable sandwich bag, which covered a newly made slit that acted as the entrance to Sam's stomach. The slit looked like the house-side of an old letter-box, with thick bristles that would guide foreign objects into the stomach. Once the object in question was in the sandwich bag, and the seal closed, an automatic vacuum device which was installed on the inside of the slit activated, causing the objects within the bag to be sucked through the slit and into the stomach. Once the objects were within Sam's stomach, it took 4 minutes for her 'power' to work. She could then use the button on her neck to induce vomiting and voila, anything that was broken in her stomach reemerged as if brand new.

After explaining all of this, Dr. Miller looked quite pleased with himself. Sam, on the other hand, looked entirely shell-shocked. All colour had been flushed from her face. She was numb. She was surely dreaming, yet she could feel the button on her neck, and see the docking station on her side. She was a monster, a lab-experiment, and she had had no say whatsoever. They had ruined her. Sam began to get hysterical, thrashing about in her cot. She managed to break her left foot from the chains that tied her down before a team of technicians entered and administered a hefty dose of sedative. She heard Miller state that *"She'd come around eventually"*, before slipping into the oblivion of unconsciousness.

• • •

It had been 11 months since the incident. It all seemed like a distorted dream now. Sam remembered that she had felt betrayed at the time. She smiled at the thought. Miller had liberated her from would have been a life of confused vomiting. He had figured out her new evolved body and ensured that she would be able to control it. He did all of that for free, well at least in the context of money. It wasn't long after the surgery when Dr. Miller had suggested that Sam join their team and allow them to put her power to use for the good of humanity. It was an enticing offer. She still remembered the look of brutal disappointment on Miller's face when she declined. Sam had been still reeling from the horror of being operated on without permission. She was too emotional then to make such a drastic commitment. She hoped maybe one day to use her power for the purposes Miller suggested, but he hadn't been in contact since she was discharged and that was over 10 months ago.

Sam hadn't stayed idle though. She'd quit her old job as a barista and started her own business. Like all new business owners, she'd been nervous about it, but Sam also had a unique gift which came in very handy in her line of business. She used absolutely no equipment in an industry that previously necessitated it. She had fundamentally changed the game and taken up 91% of the market of the city within a month of opening. Most people came for the gimmick of it all, but the real pull was that Sam was only charging €30 for a service that usually cost at least €100. Sam, using her newfound powers, had opened her very own Phone Repair Shop, and it was a massive success. All she did was put the phone, with its broken screen, into her sandwich-bag docking station, allow it to enter her stomach and wait 4 minutes. Then she'd press the button on her neck, vomit back up the phone, and it was as if brand new. At 30 quid a pop, with a four-minute repair time, people were coming from miles away just to have her repair their screens. Sam had also begun to not throw up anything besides the broken item in question. Her body was adapting to its new abilities, and so bile and stomach acid no longer came out with her vomit.

Sam had been through quite an ordeal, but had managed to pull through it all and come out on top. She was making quite a living, and a name for herself, whilst enjoying the fruits of her mutated labour. Unfortunately, normality wouldn't last long for her. Due to her unique abilities, and the nature of her relationship with Dr. Barton Miller, she would soon be dragged into a world of danger, adventure, and life-or-death vomiting. See, it hadn't happened yet, but soon Miller would undergo a freak mutation of his own, which would set him on a path to have the superhuman abilities of a stick of celery. Sam wouldn't know it until she needed to, but she'd save his life one day. Barton, whilst in the state of celery, would be chewed up by his arch nemesis Chicken Bronson. Sam would save his life using her powers, and he would be forever in her debt. But that wasn't for now. For now, Sam ran a successful phone repair service, and that was just fine.

Creepy-Spider, Hidden-Mantis

Dear children,

I remember my entire childhood. That's nothing extraordinary or exceptional, everyone around here can do that. You too will remember it all. I just note it here because there's a chance that someone else, reading this, may not be from around here, and therefore may not remember their whole childhood. I've read about different groups of peoples and entire species having very different levels of memory. Some can't even remember an hour ago, and to me, that's the weird thing. Remembering everything is just what life is for me, for us. It's not as exciting as you'd expect. My childhood was quite brief and uneventful. I remember the would-be traumas so perfectly that they never became traumas because I never misremembered them in such a way that would render them traumatic. Things happened, and I understand them fully now, in crystallised precision. Again, so does everyone else, so this is nothing outside of normal.

I have one step-brother; we share a mother. Neither of us ever met our fathers. They both left before we were born. In honesty, I don't really know many people who have ever met their dad. Most are gone before the child is born, so again, that's fairly normal too. In fact, it's quite weird if you do know your father. There's one girl, Lizzy, she has a dad, but he's not biological. He kind of took her in after her mother died. She got sucked up by the blades of a combine harvester a couple of years ago. Tragic, but not unheard of. Other than Lizzy, I don't think I know anyone with a dad around.

Mom, bless her soul, talks about dad being gone like he had a choice. Like she hadn't made him leave. Don't get me wrong, my mother is the purest heart in town, but she made my father leave, the same way she'd made Arnold's dad go away (that's my stepbrother, by the way). Mom always argues that it was biological, and it couldn't have worked any other way, but I think that's complete shite-talk. I'm sure she tells herself that so she can sleep better at night. She always says life is too short as it is to be worrying about the past. She can be very profound at times, and she's right. The point is, nobody in this town seems to have fathers, except for those fucking Spider-pricks.

Obviously, you wouldn't call them Spiders to their faces, that's just outright insulting, and it may even be racist, I'm not sure. The O'Malleys are called Spiders by everyone in town behind their backs. Spider-Malley is a general term used to refer to any particular one of the Malleys. In fairness, I get why people call them Spiders. Obviously, they look a bit different from the rest of town. I'm not being racist; I'm just telling the truth. On top of that, the fuckers always creep up behind you to say 'hello' and you'd nearly shit yourself every time. They don't do this on purpose; it's just in their nature. They're just creepy little bastards. The O'Malleys are hands down the biggest family in our community, there seems to be hundreds of them and to be honest, there's only 73 of them. I always find it *hard to tell who's who, because of the sheer quantity of them, and they all look alike (Again, not racist). They all have the same father though, and he's been around the whole time. Big John Malley, king of the Spiders. He's a hefty old fella, like a proper massive fucker. He rarely leaves the house, but whenever I catch a glimpse, he genuinely terrifies me. Luckily, he's far too big and slow to ever creep up on you. I heard he used to be a serious hunter when he was younger and was the reason the town survived a bad Famine about 50 years before I was born. The Spiders rarely talk about their dad around us, like they feel bad for having a father. It makes no difference to us though, it's kind of a cultural thing really, for us not to have fathers. It's just unheard of.*

What I don't get is why all the men in town who become fathers just disappear before the children are born. It doesn't make sense to me. I don't think I'd leave my children fatherless as I continued my life as a married bachelor elsewhere, but the evidence suggests that I will do that. Lizzy's dad is the only exception, and that doesn't really count, anyway. I just feel like I'd be relentlessly guilty for the rest of my life if I left my wife on her own to bring up our child. Right now, I can almost guarantee I will be a present father to my children, to you, but maybe that'll change. There's nothing I can think of that makes me so inherently different to every other man that I'd be the first father to remain with his kids. It's fairly sad in ways.

I'm a virgin by the way. I'm gonna assume you think that's funny, me, an adult male, a virgin. I'd be embarrassed if it weren't the absolute norm around here. I've read about other cultures, and how 'casual' sex is a thing, and it's done for pleasure rather than procreation, mostly. That seems a bit bizarre to be honest. Where I'm from, sex is used only for procre-

ation, no exceptions. This isn't a law, and nothing happens if people have sex in other circumstances, it just simply never happens. Generally, people get educated for around 12 years, then you find a wife/husband, you get married, and procreate. It seems to me, a lot more straightforward a way of living. I never truly understood why people from other places carry out the act of procreating, yet simultaneously hope that they don't conceive. Around here, that's the ultimate goal, the purest purpose of life. Well, that's what we're taught in school. However, there's a huge contradiction between procreating being the end-goal of life, and every would-be father going into exile once the deed is done. There might be something they're not telling us, or else they have simply never questioned this dogma, which is exceedingly more likely.

As it happens, I'm due to be married this afternoon. I said I'd write this brief little diary thing before then, just as proof to my future kids that I at least considered why all men leave their children. Kids, if you are reading this, and I am gone, just know that I never wanted to leave, consciously. If I'm gone, then my mother may be right, and that it is in fact, 'biological', although I have absolutely no idea what that even means to be quite frank. Perhaps after conception, there's some pheromone release that makes it biologically impossible for myself and your mother to be together. Only time will tell.

Your father,
Oscar.

• • •

The wedding went as all weddings do; too quickly. Oscar got married to his girlfriend, Tammy, in a small wooded area near the edge of town. It was a small ceremony with only close family and friends present. Once the ceremony had finished, there was an after-party in the centre of town which was open to anyone who is interested, as was tradition. Tammy and Oscar were clearly deeply in love and had been for quite some time. It was a picturesque wedding for a picturesque couple. Weddings are more than the union of two people though. Weddings also give an opportunity to the single friends of the bride and groom to meet, and perhaps, find a match of their own. In fact, this secondary function was made explicit in Oscar's culture, and a period of time was given to the singles amongst the gathering to take to the dance-floor. This section is crudely but appropriately called the 'Mating-Dance'.

Oscar was nervous, despite his matter-of-fact disposition. He was nervous about being married. He was nervous about having sex, and he was nervous about how his psychology might change after it. For these reasons, Oscar took advantage of the free time he had during the mating-dance and intentionally got way more drunk than he ever had been before. He sat at the bar for 20 minutes, drinking shot after shot with machine-like precision. His long arms making the process look like some sort of ritual dance. By the end of the mating-dance, there were very few people left at the party that were sober, but absolutely no one was near the level of intoxication that Oscar had plateaued at. He had pushed past the point of embarrassingly, sloppy drunk to an almost enlightened sense of self-awareness to the point that each time he fell, or stumbled, it looked to be an intended action. Oscar was so falsely confident that he believed he could get out of having sex, by thinking a baby into his wife. He convinced himself that he had some kind of tele-fertilization, an ability to impregnate women with his mind alone. Luckily, it was quite hard to convince Tammy of this when, mid-explanation, Oscar got sick into the half-empty pint glass he had been holding in his left hand.

Tammy led Oscar to the bar and got him some water to sober up. She wasn't angry. She actually seemed quite pleased with Oscar, or at least didn't mind that he was legless. She passed her hand over the rim of the glass before handing him the glass, but Oscar, in his inebriation, never noticed. Oscar skulled the pint of water and gestured to the bartender for another. He looked up at Tammy, who was smiling brilliantly as she surveyed the party surrounding them. Oscar, at that moment, couldn't ever imagine what would possess him to leave such a beautiful soul. That was the final thought Oscar had before he blacked out.

• • •

Tammy could already feel the weight of the pregnancy within her, even though it had only been a few hours. She felt wholesome and powerful. There was still plenty to be done to convince the town, well the male half of town, that Oscar had taken his leave. She smiled to herself. She thought it was perfectly beautiful that then men thought they ran society, that they were in charge, yet they were systematically slaughtered by the women for centuries. The men were clueless. They had no idea that falling in love for them, meant certain and eventual death. She had felt the rush of ancestral power when she had cleared Oscar's head from his shoulders. The squelch of ripping flesh had made her climax instantly. It was even more exhilarating that she had taken his head from his stupid shoulders with her bare hands. She had always liked Oscar, but he was a means to an end. A means to a child, which was now bubbling inside her.

Oscar's body was still lifeless and blood-soaked at the end of the bed, but Tammy seemed unbothered. She was focusing on a small letter she had found in their room. Oscar had written some sort of letter to his future kids about not wanting to leave. As soon as she finished reading, she ate it, both nutritious for the baby, and a practical way of destroying evidence. Nobody could read that letter as it caused doubt, which would lead to suspicion, which risked the truth coming out. The truth would be too much for the little town to handle. Only the women and the spiders knew the true nature of their existence. The men were left to their little bubble, left to think they controlled life, but they were merely puppets.

The truth was that every single father since the dawn of the species had been coldly and callously murdered by his wife, directly after insemination. The wife then either hid, or ate the body, and told the whole town that their husband had left with no explanation or reasons as to why. This was the gist of everyone's story, and it had become so normal that nobody questioned whether it was true.

This is just how things are in the life of the Praying Mantis.

The Jay-Zeus Crisis

The hangover has always, without doubt, been the worst part of drinking. The shit-talk, the vomiting, the embarrassment; they have all come second to the sheer dirtiness of the hang. It has so many layers. The dryness, the headaches, the inability to drink water, the anxiety, the self-hate. It is by far the worst part of drinking. Hangovers, as you know, are intensified the longer the bender. In the case of our pal Jay, he'd just come off a very long, and very strange three-day drinking session. Not to be dramatic, but this particular session may have changed the entire course of human history. Hangovers get a little more surreal and angry when you're in your 30s, as Jay found out on this palpable Sunday morning.

The weekend had started on Thursday, with himself and the boys heading to their favourite spot for some food and a wicked amount of alcohol. The boys loved to make a long weekend even longer by taking the Friday off with a bank-holiday Monday on the far side of Sunday. This weekend was even more special, as it was Jay's Stag-Do. He was marrying the lovely Mary, who all the lads thought was too good for Jay, but never said. The night started like every other night, with a large meal, accompanied by several bottles of wine. They always drank wine to begin with, but it

41

was rare that anyone ever finished the night on the stuff. Jay got on with most of the group, except for one of them. He'd kinda entered the group on the tails of one of the other lads, but Jay didn't really know much about him. He also tried to abbreviate his name to 'Jay' which pissed our Jay right off, as he'd been called Jay since he was a toddler. Our Jay's middle name was Zeus, due to his mother being absolutely obsessed, to the level of sickness, with anything to do with Gods and Deities. Sometimes people just called him Zeus, but he really preferred Jay. The other Jay was a bit obnoxious as well, always grasping for attention, and was clearly very jealous of the way the group naturally looked to our Jay for leadership. Jay didn't try to exclude him, though, and made sure that everyone was having a good night as much as possible. Our Jay, by far, made the most money out of the lads. He was a fairly successful architect, renowned in the country for his ability to make sturdy, reliable houses from wood. On top of that, he was well known for his charity work and helping the sick, so it was quite common for restaurant owners to offer free courses, as a sort of PR move. Jay never neglected to take advantage of the free offers from kind strangers, although this more often than not, caused him to get incredibly intoxicated on the free booze that various establishments provided him. The lads were always on the ball with finding ways to bring up embarrassing stories of Jay's drunken escapades, especially when his girlfriend Mary was around. Their all-time favourite story to tell was about the time Jay got black-out drunk at a wedding and convinced himself that he had somehow converted water into red-wine. Himself and his date for the evening (his mother!) were quickly escorted from the premises, but Jay didn't remember any of that and denied any evidence of it actually happening.

The Thursday night was quite uneventful in terms of the weekend, but it was the only night Jay could actually remember. They stayed in a bar called 'Pass(Hang)over' (Jewish owned) for the whole night and enjoyed a good night, gorging on the food and drink that was in abundance. He remembered the other Jay being very quiet all night, and he even left early. However, this was more of a relief than a worry to Jay as he always felt a little on edge around the awkward outsider. Friday started early, with a few crisp cans directly after waking up. The session never slowed down from then until about 4am Sunday morning.

Jay remembered nothing after about 6:17pm Friday night. He blacked out after the 4th bottle of wine. Peter had been shoving glass, after glass of red wine into Jay's hand all day. After all, it was his Stag weekend, and he had no excuses not to be hammered. Waking up Sunday morning, Jay had no idea that nobody had seen him since Friday night. He'd spent the entirety of Saturday incognito. Off the grid. Jay's first and most prominent clue that something very strange had happened on his 4-day Stag was finding himself waking up in a very cold, and very dark, cave. What was even weirder was that he was lying on an almost perfectly rectangular stone slab, which was raised off the ground by another, smaller cube of solid rock beneath it. It looked like a hipster coffee table you'd buy at Ikea, although Jay had no idea what Ikea was, and these tables wouldn't be available in bulk for at least another 2,000 years. Still, Jay found himself waking up on this Ikea-coffee-table -looking stone slab in a cave. There were splinters of light outlining a small enough stone, which was blocking a small enough opening in the wall of the cave. The opening looked big enough for Jay to crawl comfortably through though. Jay was quite scrawny but had one of those skinny-6-packs that doesn't really count. Jay was the type that believed he was shredded though, rather than accepting that he struggled to put on any weight. He got onto the floor and assumed the position of a sultry, bottom-dwelling crab with his hands and forearms taking the brunt of his weight. This allowed him to kick out the small rock which blocked the crawl-space with unexpected finesse. Jay crawled out into the sunlight of a warm, Sunday morning. The dull ache of three days on the batter pounded against the back of his eyes.

The Stag had taken place in a small town about 30 minutes from the city where Jay and the boys lived. Considering Jay's growing popularity, it made sense to keep the Stag as low-key as possible. This clinical level of planning was, of course, Peter's idea and it now worked in Jay's favour, as the lads were sure to be within the bounds of the small town, making them easy enough to find. The cave was a short distance from the town, and he could see the small cluster of buildings ahead of him.

If Jay was honest, Peter was the brains behind nearly all the groups' greatest ploys. He was the reason Jay had decided to become an architect, as well as the mastermind behind the PR strategy that had brought Jay into the spotlight of the public. Although Jay held all the charisma and suaveness of a great leader, without Peter, he'd still be living with his mother and his step-dad. Peter was the real talent, and the guilt of leaving him in the shadows hounded Jay every time he was hungover, and Jay was hungover quite a lot.

Jay took his time walking back into town from the cave he woke up in. Aside from being absolutely shook from the weekend, it was a nice morning, and he was enjoying the nourishing sunlight, as it lapped at him across the small inland lake. All it took was a light breeze from the East to inform Jay that something was very, very wrong. Usually, any type of air movement caused his glorious beard to shake and sway in tandem with it. Jay had been growing out his beard since before it was cool since he was 19 years old. However, on this fatal morning, there was no shaking, there was no feeling of unsettled hair. Jay quickly reached for his beard and felt nothing 3 inches below his chin. To his terror, his chin and jaw, where once was covered in luscious brown-amber curls, was now layered with an uneven, sloppy stubble. Jay fell to his knees in anguish by the edge of the lake he was walking alongside and gazed into his own eyes reflecting back at him from the surface of the water. His face was unrecognisable. The only person alive that could have recognised him was his mother. Jay had been bearded with long flowing hair ever since he had met the crew. Now, he had scruffy stubble. His head had also been bluntly shaved. Jay guessed it was a two blade job, although blade measurements and electric razors wouldn't be invented for another 1900 years. On top of that, his face was gaunt and stretched from dehydration and not having eaten in over 24 hours. His eyes were wild from hunger. Jay's appearance held no resemblance to the man who had left for his Stag on that overcast Thursday afternoon. He looked like a fella who would approach you asking for money for a hostel; untrustworthy and unpleasant.

Jay was distraught. His entire identity had been built around his glorious locks and gravity-defying beard. He couldn't remember a thing about the day previous, but could only assume this had been a decision he'd made in his inebriated state. He knew none of the lads would ever attempt this type of prank, not again. 3 years previously, Jay's cousin John had come at him with scissors, threatening to cut his hair off if he didn't put his head under the water when they were swimming. John's blatant joke didn't resonate well with Jay and was met with a crisp and clear left puck to John's jaw. After that, nobody had tried to mess with Jay's hair ever again, but he did eventually put his head under the water.

Jay rose from his knees. He was in severe emotional turmoil. Losing his hair and beard combo had hit him like a hot truck going 90 on a highway in Lost Angeles. Jay didn't even know what a highway, or a truck, or what Los Angeles was, but these were the emotions he was feeling. He continued on his way back towards town, with tears building behind his eyes.

He heard the boys before he saw them. They must have started drinking straight after waking again because they were loud and unified. The ruckus was coming from the square in the centre of the small town. As Jay walked into the square, the noise continued. None of the boys recognised him. I mean, why would they? He looked nothing like the man they had known the last 3 or so years. Jay walked towards them, trying to join in with the banter as best he could. The 12 lads embraced his presence the same way anyone would embrace a stranger; politely, but quietly wishing the strange man would leave. They were sitting at a long table on the outdoor patio of a nearby bar. Jay pulled up a stool and continued to join in, disrupting the ebb and flow of the conversation. The 12 lads allowed this to go on for 15 minutes until Peter, Jay's BFF, finally plucked up the courage and asked simply

'Who the fuck are you, fella?'

A hush fell over the table. They had been so loud, and the silence so sudden, that regular pedestrians nearby stopped to see what was going on. Jay looked around nervously. Nobody had recognised him. There was a good chance none of the pricks had even realised that he had been gone, or that he woke up in a cave that morning. Eventually, Jay responded with a very passive-aggressive:

"You know who I am."

The look of confusion on Peter's brown face changed slowly to one of surprise, to a hysterical fit of laughter. This realization spread around the table like a Mexican wave, until every single one of them was laughing inconsolably. By now, Jay had gone crimson read and started slugging on a canister of wine that had been left out on the table. Slowly, the laughter began to die down, and the group began chanting "Jay-Zeus has Risen" over and over again. Peter threw his arm around Jay and recanted the tale of the weekend, how Jay had gone missing late Friday night, but they decided he'd turn up eventually as he always did. The shock of

Jay's new appearance wore off quickly, but the lads began the chant randomly throughout the day, and for the days to come. Passers-by had no idea what was going on, other than the fact that a man named Jay-Zeus had risen from somewhere.

Due to all the commotion, and the return of Jay-Zeus, nobody had noticed other-Jay slip off. The entire weekend had been an ordeal for him. He wasn't fond of the lads, and he certainly detested Jay. He walked back to the hotel, oddly happy with himself, which was out of character. He strolled up to reception to check out.

Other-Jay: I'd like to check-out, please.

Receptionist: No problem, sir. And what is the name used to book the room?

Other-Jay: Ja…

He paused. He had almost forgotten that he'd used his full name to book the room.

Other-Jay: Eh, Judas. It should be under Judas.

Receptionist: Excellent Mr. Judas. Will that be everything?

Judas: Oh I borrowed this yesterday, they said to drop it back into you this morning before I left.

Judas slid a cut-throat razor, traditionally used for shaving, across the counter and made his way for the door. Jay-Zeus would undoubtedly figure out what happened eventually and say that Judas had betrayed him, the melodramatic prick. It was only a small prank, but it still made Judas feel damn good about getting one back on Jay, their beloved leader.

Judas left for home. It would all blow over within the week, and he could hang with the lads again. There was no way Jay would hold a grudge. There was no way anyone who heard them chanting 'Jay-Zeus has risen' would take the chant out of context and start spreading rumours. There was no way such a small event could get way out of hand, be taken completely out of context, distorted, and remembered for say…. The next 2,000 years.

Do You Know The Capital of Georgia?

(inspired by a real conversation)

Daragh: I told you I didn't wanna learn anything new. I'm finished with it, my learning days are over!

Sqweeker: By profession I'm required to teach, so it's gonna leak out sometimes.

Davin: It's Tbilisi.

Daragh: Tibiscuits?

Sqweeker: No the capital of Georgia is Tbilisi.

Davin: I told you, you didn't know it.

Daragh: And I told you I didn't wanna know. It's useless.

Sqweeker: It has one of those 't's that sounds like it's in the wrong place though? Tbilisi (laughs).

Daragh: Yeah okay… My name has two silent letters in it, and it really grinds my gears.

Davin: So you're saying it's not pronounced Dara-guh-huh?

Sqweeker: It was up until the 80s no?

Daragh: (laughs) no, the 'GH' is silent.

Davin: That's a fairly loud D at the beginning though.

Sqweeker: And the R is really loud. It's the type of loud that makes the neighbours call over around 11:30 and ask if you could keep it down.

Davin: I dunno, that D is pretty damn loud. Still modest though, like it's loud but would make sure to be quiet after 10pm.

Daragh: Here can we not discuss the linguist content of my name, I was just saying there were two silent letters is all.

Sqweeker: So it's not pronounced Dara-guh-huh?

Daragh: No! To be fair it was briefly pronounced Dara-Gee-Hah in 2001, but that got reversed as soon as the whole 9/11 thing happened, the name sounded too terrorist-y for public consumption so it went back to being just Da-ra.

Davin: I think I read that somewhere.

Daragh: Sham, no you didn't coz I just made that up.

Davin: Oh yeah… I was born without 'dis' anyway.

Daragh: …what?

Davin: 'Dis' doesn't apply to me like, I don't have it.

Daragh: Please explain what you're on about?? (laughs)

Davin: Well like, mom says I'm intellectually abled, I have an intellectual ability. There's no 'dis'.

Daragh: Right…

Davin: The doctor said I have a social ability too which is actually unreal.

Daragh: Dav I think you might-

Sqweeker: Man, leave it. He knows.

Daragh: Are you sure?

Sqweeker: No honestly I've told him a few times already. He knows.

Davin: Sure me and Sqweek have conversations all the time in our heads.

Sqweeker: And don't you hear them too Daz?

Daragh: Eh, I guess…

Sqweeker: Don't you sit with a glass of bourbon and watch me in your head talk to Dav whilst also sipping a glass of bourbon?

Daragh: Ehmm…

Davin: It's nothing to worry about me and Sqweek do it all the time, it's how most of our creative stuff comes about, just listening to each other think.

Daragh: Right?

Sqweeker: And sure all your creative stuff comes from that interaction, you get your ideas from what me and Dav talk about, and you can hear it in your head. We're like a devil and an angel on your shoulders except-…

Daragh: Except neither of ye are swayed either way good or bad ye're just strange?

Sqweeker: Exactly! (laughs) *Sips from can of Coors Light. The Rocky Mountain Freshness seal isn't blue, and so the can isn't cooled to serving coldness but Sqweeker doesn't seem to mind.

Daragh: Does this mean I have multiple personalities?

Davin: I suppose it does yeah, in ways.

Daragh: But there's a big problem with that isn't there?

Davin: Already stigmatising yourself? You won't last long.

Daragh: No I mean, wouldn't our personalities have to differ dramatically for multiple personality disorder to be involved? We're all very similar, we're all fairly weird, like.

Sqweeker: (laughs) Yeah I suppose we are but how else do you explain the mind thing?

Daragh: Are you two not just duplicates of me? Or different versions of me? And we're all somehow independent of each other? Like I don't think I control what you two say?

Davin: I would hope not!

Sqweeker: Daz I don't think you've anything to worry about we're just friends who drink together and sometimes you can hear us think.

Daragh: Actually, why are you drinking right now??

Sqweeker: Are ye not?

Davin: I am.

Daragh: Well hardly, considering where I am!

Davin: So dramatic.

Daragh: If I was drinking here it would raise all sorts of trouble for us- I mean me, and plus it's the middle of the day!

Sqweeker: Sure it's only a few cans we're not saying you have to, myself and Dav will drive it on.

Daragh: Lads do ye ever think how weird people would think we are if they heard some of our conversations? They're very gas like.

Davin: I imagine some people have heard AND do think we're weird. Weird is good though, better than being normal.

Sqweeker: Will you give that cliché a rest sham, it's very drawn out.

Daragh: What do you mean Sqweek?

Sqweeker: Well like these days everyone claims to be weird, and that normal is boring, so if everyone is as weird as they say, then being weird IS normal, and so everyone is actually normal and boring…

Daragh: (laughs) You've thought about that in far too much detail!

Sqweeker: I'm just saying, it's the ones that don't claim to be 'weird in a good way' that you need to watch out for, they're the real weirdos.

Davin: Good point, well made *swigs can*

Daragh: So are we weird or normal?

Davin: Oh well me and Sqweeker are definitely strange, so are you in fairness but you can mask it. People don't know straight away with you.

Daragh: But didn't we just confirm we're all the same person?

Sqweeker: Did we? I can't say there's any evidence for that. We're all the same weird but sure we can't be the same person. For example, I think it's okay to be drinking right now but you're up on your high horse about it.

Daragh: And other people know you two a well?

Davin: Ehh yeah! Jesus, Dee, we're not fucking imaginary!

Daragh: I'm just saying I've never seen other people around when I'm chatting to you two.

Sqweeker: Well we could say the same about you Daz, maybe you're imaginary?

Daragh: Hold on, I'm always here!

Davin: Nah man, whenever me and Sqweeker are with a different person you're nowhere to be seen. Won't even snap us back either ya pelic.

Daragh: I suppose if I've never seen ye with other people then it makes sense that you've not seen me…

Sqweeker: You can't always be in control mate.

Daragh: I never said I had to be.

Davin: We know.

Sqweeker: The point is, all three of us are always here, but one of us is always a little bit more here. Like right now, you're surrounded by other people, me and Dav aren't, we're just here drinking. Sure you can chat away to us whenever, but you're the one who's good at masking us up, so you're usually the one in control.

Davin: I can't believe how often we need to explain the dynamics of this to you Daz.

Sqweeker: Nobody thinks you're weird Dee, but when me and Dav get out there, people start to wonder. Luckily for you it's mainly when we're drunk so people write it off as a drunk thing, but we all know the real reason you change.

Daragh: I told you I don't want to learn anymore.

Davin: This isn't learning pal, you're just re-remembering.

Daragh: Just stop.

Sqweeker: Okay we'll ease up, but eventually you'll have to come to terms with it.

Daragh: We've already wasted enough time here; What did you say the capital of Georgia was again?

Dav and Sqweeker: Tbilisi!

Daragh: Sound lads, this geography test is way harder than I thought it was gonna be.

Eavesdropping in the Dark

Have you ever considered how inherently random your entire life is? Have you ever questioned why you'd feel a deep shame if you found yourself outside with no pants on? Or why you feel an unignorable urge to fit-in, to be liked by those around you? Most people haven't, and those of us that have considered these things usually tend to bury such thoughts as they bring about a mental discomfort that's hard to shake, and even harder to explain. Yet, it's something that always played on Brandon's mind. He always found himself wondering why everything we did was done in that specific way. This type of thought process naturally led him to become quite socially awkward, as his actions portrayed this sense of questioning, becoming more and more contra to the norm as time went on. He hadn't become a social outlier or anything like that, but rather everyone who knew him sensed there was something a little off. Some found this aspect of his personality endearing, others found it to be the reason he could never totally accept another person. Either way, thoughts of how frivolous social norms were always stuck to his brain, the way freshly chewed gum sticks to long hair.

One such idea that always captivated him was shopping centres. He never truly understood how people spent hours there, and it bothered him even more that such people never questioned what they were up to. He always argued that spending money at shopping centres, on non-essential items, was a guaranteed way of becoming trapped in a cycle of never having enough money to do anything you'd presumably consider worthwhile. You'd spend the money, which you've made working for a capitalist system, on buying items back from the same exact system. You'd essentially be paying the system for allowing you to work for them so that you could buy random products from other outlets. This thought alone frustrated him to his very core. He remembered spending hours when he was young waiting for his mother in various shopping centres. He'd just stand at some balcony, or sit in a coffee outlet, watching the hundreds of people flocking to retail outlets, to give their hard earned money back to the system that had paid it to them. He could never get around the idea that it was some sort of trickery. That somewhere along the line, we'd been corrupted into thinking that this was the way we wanted to live.

That isn't to say Brandon boycotted this way of living. In a sense, we have no choice but to live this way. He also didn't want to be labelled a freak, so he'd find himself in town, or Mahon Point the occasional Saturday evening, meeting friends, or a girl for some classic, social interface. Brandon was in Cork City centre this one Saturday. It was a dry April evening, warm enough to just be wearing a t-shirt. The first day of the year this could happen, really. The sun wasn't out, but it was warm and humid. He could feel the sun pressing down on the light grey clouds, the same way a marble presses down on a lightly tensioned bedsheet; its presence felt but unseen. He'd been in to meet a few friends for the Ireland match and a few day-pints. He'd had 5 crisp pints of Fosters, and so there was an electric haze coursing around his body and mind, unlocking thoughts he'd not thought of in a while, while simultaneously causing his mind to believe everyone thought he was the shit. It's the best stage of becoming drunk. Two more pints and he'd be talking shite to anyone who'd listen, slurring as he did so. Right now, Brandon had complete control over his mind's actions, while still having a suave, confident air about him.

As he walked along Grand Parade, Brandon heard snippets of several conversations as variously sized groups passed by him. He always found this sort of cocktail-party listening quite amusing, as you'd get just a tiny shard of the conversation, with little or no context to what the topic of conversation was. Two student-girls walked by and Brandon heard the phrase,

'… and the stupid bastard doesn't even know.'

A couple walked past shortly after that and all Brandon heard was a high-pitched wail, followed by a small woman playfully pushing her much taller boyfriend. As he turned the corner of Grand Parade onto South Mall two lads walked by and one of them floated the phrase,

'…she'd empty yer bag for sure.'

It sauntered into the air with a song-like quality. These little splurges of conversation indulged Brandon's imagination regularly, allowing him to playfully recreate the context around the very small sample of chat he could extract from passers-by. Brandon often came to town, or to Mahon Point alone, just to feast on such snippets of conversation. It allowed him to exercise his imagination in ways no other activity could. He often found himself in a deep sense of flow during these outings, eventually awaking from his world of imagination to find that hours had past. On this particular occasion, the enjoyable sensation was amplified by the 5 delicious pints he'd allowed himself earlier that afternoon. The serotonin zoomed around the neurons of his cerebral cortex frantically as he imagined the multitude of possibilities that could possibly have arisen to make a man in his mid-twenties concoct the words 'she'd empty yer bag'. His brain was consumed by this indulgent activity as he walked down the South Mall. Brandon was so consumed by this outlandish activity that he began to cross the road without looking for cars. He had no awareness of the world around him. Instead, Brandon was fixated on the imaginary narrative that was unfolding between his ears. He created the idea that there was a woman in this man's life that could empty a spice-bag within seconds of it coming into her possession. That, of course, made no sense, as you couldn't get a spice-bag in Cork. Still, the superhuman ability of this woman to empty this man's bag in seconds overwhelmed his frontal lobe.

Brandon was lucky; there were no cars coming. He hadn't even noticed the qualitative difference that exists between walking on the concrete of the footpath and walking on the warm tarmac of the South Mall. He didn't notice the frantic screams of caution that came from several passers-by, not consciously anyway. However he did hear the very imminent, very nearby, abrupt horn of a Bus Eireann bus, but not until it was far too late. He looked up in time to notice that it was the 215. His last thought before its impact was that this bus used to be the number 10, just before the Recession. He also had the thought that this bus wouldn't be needed at all if it weren't for the capitalist greed of our hopeless society. He remembered contemplating the irony of this whole situation. He'd hated the whole idea of capitalist-shopping culture for his entire life, and now it appeared that his life would be stolen away by a bus whose only purpose was to shuttle people to and from these very shopping centres. Those were Brandon's very last thoughts before the bus collided with him, sending his limp body skidding 30 feet down the South Mall.

There's something eerily reassuring about the consistent, melodic repetitiveness of a heart monitoring machine. Each new beep brings with it the soft affirmation that the person remains alive. Beep. Beep. Beep. Brandon couldn't see, or feel anything. He assumed his eyes were closed but couldn't be sure. It felt the same way dreaming does. You know you're asleep but you can't prove it, or know where your body is, because the motor and sensory cortices of your brain are shut down. He wasn't dreaming right now though. He was awake to the extent that Brandon was aware of himself, but had no physical awareness of his body. He couldn't tell if he was in pain, where he was, what position he was in. To be honest, Brandon wasn't even sure he was alive. He considered the possibility that he was now in the nothingness; the afterlife. That idea fell short when he realized again that he could hear the heart monitor, which in turn meant he had ears and that they were working. What was confusing though, is that Brandon couldn't always hear the heart monitor. It came and went in dribs and drabs, the same way music comes through earphones with a faulty jack-connection. It was erratic and imperfect, but it was still very reassuring. It meant he hadn't died. Brandon could remember it all, in precise clarity now. The man shouting at him to watch out for the bus, followed by the bus driver airing his horn. He even remembered the look of anguish on the bus driver's face as he realised the brakes wouldn't stop the bus in time. And now this. This strange new reality, in between sleep and wakefulness. He was alive but had no way of being able to express this life. Brandon was undead.

'Jesus fucking Christ'

The words jumped into his awareness and were gone again, the same way the heart monitor was coming in and out. It was his father's voice. Himself and the mother must have been in the room, or had entered just recently. Brandon wondered if they'd told Mia what happened. She was living in Adelaide in Oz. She'd probably be on the next flight home once she heard, pure melodramatic like that. His mom was no doubt up in a heap as well, blaming herself even though she had no hand in what had happened whatsoever. Brandon wanted to scream to them. He wanted them to know he was here, that he was alright. They could probably only see his lifeless body, which was probably looking more than a little beaten up, and wondering whether he could hear them or not. He could, at least partly anyway, and he wished that he could comfort them. Brandon wished he could take the piss out of the pair of them, in a way that told them he loved them, in his own little psychopathic way, but he was left in isolated silence once again.

Beep. Beep. Beep

The heart monitor again, this time with no accompanying voices. Had his parents already left? They just gotten here? Unless time was passing at a very different pace, it seemed like he'd heard dad's voice just a few minutes ago. Brandon felt hurt that they'd left so quickly. They could have at least played with the idea that he was able to hear them.

'Oh my god, you absolute eejit.'

Those words. The half Cork, half Australian accent. She'd only been gone six months and was already losing her accent. Still, as always, a complete sausage. His sister. How did she get here so fast? It usually takes her the bones of 2 days to get home from Oz, and mom and dad had only just found out about me, by the sounds of dad's reaction. How much time had passed in what seemed like a few short minutes? Brandon began to wonder how many people had actually come to visit him, compared to how many people he'd actually heard talking out loud near him. It seemed that Brandon could only hear snippets of sounds, and that the segments of silence in between didn't adhere to the rules of time people were normally used to. These little sound bites of upset family and friends were all Brandon had to comfort him while trapped in this purgatory.

Initially, most occurrences of sound were a combination of the reassuring heart monitor combined with some arbitrary half-sentence of a familiar voice. As always, Brandon imagined what conversation was being constructed around these sound bites, and this decreased the growing sense of worry that he would never escape from this harrowing new existence. He'd spent countless hours listening in on people in real life, and now his entire existence was this twisted form of eavesdropping. The sinister reality of his life touched playfully on his mind. With no way of knowing how much time had passed, Brandon fixated on concocting these full conversations, instead of confronting the inevitability of his situation. It wasn't long however, until Brandon stopped hearing voices. Each new soundbite was an isolated portion of the heart monitor ticking away. It wasn't until the 6th consecutive occurrence of the lonely heart monitor that Brandon realised what was happening; people had stop coming to visit him. Brandon was overwhelmed with sadness, he thought, but had no way of outwardly expressing this emotion. His rational brain concluded that he must have been in the state he was for a substantial period of time if it had stopped people from visiting his lifeless body. People must have given up hope that he would ever recover. This thought should have upset Brandon, but he couldn't express this emotion, and thus, could not feel anything. He simply observed and waited for new sound bites, to see if any more information could be uncovered.

The next nine sound bites consisted of the same lonely bleep of the machine which notified that he was still alive. Occasionally, it was accompanied by the hollow sound of footsteps, as nurses and doctors walked about the corridors of the hospital Brandon assumed he was in. Brandon had more or less given up hope on anyone ever visiting him again. In fairness, the visits had begun to cause him more frustration and pain than comfort, as the reality of his inability to communicate had set in. He wished more than anything to be able to talk to his family, to be able to feel his own limbs. Yet, he remained in this limbo-existence, completely helpless.

One day (Brandon couldn't be sure how much time had passed since he had began this new life) a familiar voice accompanied the heart monitor. The sound bites had become so infrequent now that Brandon could only make out partial words of sentences

'…two year… insura… support.'

This snippet asked more questions than it answered for Brandon. Had he been under for 2 years? I hadn't felt that long for him but he had already considered that time may be skewed for him. Who was the doctor talking to and what was it about? Before he could figure it out, another sound bite interrupted his thoughts.

'No… gone… terminate… life…'

It was his dad, but he sounded different. He was no longer the confident demeanour Brandon had known. He sounded defeated and scared. He hadn't heard his mom's voice at all which meant his dad had come alone. From growing up, Brandon knew that his mother never went with his dad when tough decisions had to be made. When they'd moved from Waterford to Cork, Brandon's father went alone to his school to inform the principle they were pulling Brandon out. His mother could never face confrontation, and she wasn't here now either. If Brandon had control of his body, he would have been blinking back tears. He forced everything within himself to try to scream for help, to let his dad know he was okay and that he wasn't gone.

But nothing happened. Nothing ever happened again. There were no new sound bites. There was no reassuring heart monitor. There was nothing, endless nothing.

Sausage Titanic

It was a Friday evening. Or maybe it was a Saturday night. It was definitely a weekend night, anyway. I remember that because I remember the warm feeling of not having a tap to do the next morning. It was gonna be a pure sleep-til-12 morning, get-up-at-3 type of day. Sure it doesn't matter what day it was, the whole situation went to shit in the end, anyway.

Dry January is a scary idea for an Irish fella like myself. Usually you'd spend one night of the weekend on the sauce, one night recovering, and then it's back to Monday, back to responsibility. For whatever reason, the start of every new year begins with a collective guilt about our own drinking, and the year begins with 3 to 6 weeks of trying to stay off the gargle. I'd read an article before about a fella in Clare genuinely going insane before because he tried to stay off the drink for more than a week. He ended up going down to the local, ordering a pint and then lit the gaf on fire. He burned to death in the fire slurping away on his last ever pint. The fucked up part was he'd gotten his simple brother to lock all the doors from the outside so that nobody else could escape. When I'd first read that I was convinced it was a Waterford Whisperers creation, but I actually saw it on JOE so knew it had to be some way legitimate. Imagine losing your mind because you stayed off the beer? Surely that fella was a raging alcoholic. The lads any myself only got on the devil's water once, maybe twice a week.

Anyway, Dry January is what we were attempting. It never lasts, but the effort is always there initially. This weekend was the first weekend in the cycle of staying off the batter, so me and the lads were determined not to go out. This, however, left us with a problem, like it did every other year; what the fuck were we gonna get up to for the night? There's a weird thing about Irish drinking culture that nobody really acknowledges. We're all happy out to spend 70 euro on drink on a given night out, but fuck me there's not a chance we'll be happy to spend a tenner on a sober activity. That'd be 'a waste of money' says your average Irish eejit. That being what it is, it's quite difficult to motivate the lads to spend money on something that doesn't end with being hammered buying kebabs at 3 in the morning.

There were only three of us about for the night. Lar (His real name is Lawrence), Mayo (Erick's second name was Mayes so everyone called him Mayo), and myself (my name is Erick as well, and I was lucky enough to be the one to keep my actual name). Josh and Carpet were both busy for the night. Josh had gone home to Leitrim for the weekend and Carpet had a date or something. It was just myself Lar and Mayo in for the night. It was absolutely pelting down outside. It was the type of rain that sounded as if it would break the windows if it were allowed to continue, pure sore rain. The lads got home from work around 6:40pm. It must have been a Friday so because the lads didn't work weekends. I'd a day off so I was already after a day of doing absolutely nothing. We were all adamant about not going out, very supportive of each other we were.

Lar suggested we get a few joints rolled and watch a movie. It wasn't a bad idea, and technically it adhered to the strict rules of dry January; there were no by-laws about weed smoke, we just weren't meant to have alcohol. Mayo said he'd wait until we had at least one joint in us before ordering the pizza. We didn't even have to discuss what type of pizza to get, we all knew the suss. As we had done countless times before, Mayo would log onto the online portal for Dominoes and order one of those meal deal yokes with the pizza with all the meat on it. No chance of anything vegan going on here, not in this house. Lar was by far the best at rolling so we left him to get to work. He was a masterclass in fairness to him. It was a pity that his skill couldn't be appreciated by the public eye, not yet anyway. Carpet was always belting on about how the days of legalised weed were imminent and that it would change everything forever. Carpet was gas out. He talked and acted like the biggest stoner of the 21st century but I'd never actually seen him take a pull of a joint. He always had himself an excuse.

As talented as Lar was at rolling joints, he took his time doing it. 35 minutes had passed before he'd finished rolling 3 stellar, fat jintys. By then, my stomach was screaming at me, thinking of the amount of food it would soon consume. While Lar was rolling, myself and Mayo had picked out a movie to watch. I was easy going and Mayo insisted that we watch This Is The End. I'd seen it a few times before, but Mayo was adamant.

"It's absolutely hilarious and the actors play themselves in the movie, it's pure meta". Lar hadn't seen it before and Mayo had peaked his interest. I didn't give a fuck really, I was just happy to be doing something with other people. I'd spent the day in bed trying to figure out a way to make a quick buck. Instead I spent about 80 quid on Asos online. The sales are unbelievable. I hooked up the laptop to the TV with an HDMI cable and found a good link for the movie. Seth Rogen, James Franco and the boys. I'd always wanted to make a similar movie with the lads but sure nobody would fucking watch that. None of us are famous and half the world would need to put subtitles on to understand us, it would never work. Lar sparked up the first of the joints and Mayo began and finished the quick process of ordering the pizza. The last time we'd done this we said we'd take the hit and set-up an account for ourselves. It delayed the arrival of our pizza that time but we figured it would save us time in the long run, and by God were we right. As the joint was passed around amongst the three of us, the warm, comforting haze of highness overwhelmed my brain, as the THC activated various parts of my prefrontal cortex. If you've ever been under the influence of marijuana, you'll be familiar with the sensation of your conscious mind drifting 6 or 7 inches above where it normally resides. This is a part of the high that I always get fascinated with because it seems like your head just expanded. When I was younger, I thought it was coz the smoke caused your mind to drift to the top of your brain, the same way heat rises when you've the fire going. It's probably not a bad call to mention here that I was a complete eejit of a young fella. It wasn't long before I became one with the couch I was oozing into and I hoped t'fuck I wouldn't have to get up for the doorbell. In fairness, the two lads smoked a lot more frequently than me so their tolerance for the stuff was way stronger. Mayo was still pottering around the place doing a few bits so that he wouldn't have to get up for the night. He was in the kitchen when the doorbell chimed, and I heard the deliberate and urgent change of his direction towards the front door. I breathed a sigh of relief and further amalgamated myself with the couch. The worn leather was an ample host for my THC-ridden bag-of-black-pudding of a body.

Mayo hurried in with our feast. Lar's eyes met mine and you could almost see the saliva rising inside his mouth. He was slightly overweight, and he'd gotten into the habit of undoing his belt when he ate so that he could 'be meal-comfortable'. None of us were fans of this new behaviour. One large pizza, all the meat, two sides and a cold can of coke each. We didn't waste any time getting stuck in. The next few minutes passed in silence, aside from the dialogue of the movie (which was gas) and the odd moan of satisfaction every now and then. Nobody addressed the rising tension in the room. Nobody wished to acknowledge the conflict that had caused so much kerfuffle in the past. Not one of us dared to ask who would claim the last slice of the pizza. The last slice had earned the nickname of 'Titanic' in our gaf, and for good reason.

The Titanic slice was names thusly, as it had the power to sink and destroy any enjoyable night by just existing. It probably should have been called The Iceberg, but we were high when we came up with the name. Life would simply direct us into the last slice's existence, and it would wreak havoc on us. The last slice never became an issue when there was an even number of us sharing, because the pizza divided evenly. However, when there were three of, which there was that night, you could be sure pizza-induced anarchy was only around the corner. This little piece of pizza, the Titanic, has been the source of countless debates, arguments and feuds in the house for as long as we can remember. If you ask me, the last slice shouldn't be that big of a deal, but the lads maintain it's more about what the Titanic represents. It's prestigious, it's symbolic. It essentially means that whoever gets that piece is the alpha, if you read into that sort of thing.

Anyway, we were making our way through the pizza. Each slice taken acting to enhance the desire for that last slice. I noticed nobody had said anything in quite some time.

Me: Story with the Titanic anyway lads?

Simultaneously, both Lar and Mayo jolted their eyes in my direction, both of their faces had a look of pure desperation in them. Since this whole Titanic business had started, Lar seemed to believe he had some divine birth right to it. Everyone else agreed Lar was a sausage. Mayo on the other hand, Mayo was a contender that needed to be taken seriously. A couple of months back Mayo disappeared right in the middle of pizza time which was bizarre altogether. He returned a few minutes later absolutely drenched to the bone in a complete panic, saying that the fossette for the shower had broken and water was spewing everywhere. Of course we all rushed out into the bathroom to see what the craic was. There was no fossette broken. Mayo had soaked himself with the shower head, used the fossette as an excuse to get us away from the pizza, and claimed the Titanic piece for himself. We all re-entered the living room to find Mayo slouched on the soaking wet couch, laughing manically to himself. Carpet didn't talk to Mayo for two months after that happened. The contest for the Titanic piece was nothing to be joked about.

The tension is the room could be equated to the tension you feel around your waist when you're bursting for a piss; uncomfortable and impossible to ignore. Lar slowly took another slice from the box, never taking his eyes off of me for a second. There were only two slices left now. The Titanic could have been either of them, and Mayo had one slice in hand to take. I'd seen bigger slices before but there were 2 and half pieces of pepperoni and a circle of Cumberland sausage already on it. My mouth was filling with water.

Mayo: Look lads, we all know tis my turn to take the last piece so let's not make this into an argument.

Fuck you Mayo. If there was anyone definitely not getting that delightful Titanic it was this fucker. He'd deceived us before and there was no doubt in my mind that he'd try something again down the line. I could see Lar had come to the same conclusion in his own head and I watched as his eyes shifted around the room trying to find a way to stop Mayo. The pizza-cutter glinted in his peripheral vision. The THC coursing through his brain had made the association between the sharp pizza cutter and stopping Mayo at all costs. The mad fucker. Before I could even attempt to stop him, he'd yanked the cutter from underneath the pizza box and made one, strong, purposeful arc across the neck of

Mayo. Mayo looked to be in a state of shock first, but then started laughing as he realised nothing had happened. As his laughing became more frantic, a thin seam of red appeared on his neck, the same way Nutella seeps out from between two rice cakes if you push down on them. His neck began gushing deep crimson human-juice all over Lar and the rest of the pizza. He was dead on the couch before he could even moan about it.

It was pure quiet for a minute after that. Lar had rightly bottled it now. He looked over at me, pale as a ghost, still holding the pizza-cutter in his right, half a slice of pizza in the left.

Lar: You can't tell anyone this happened Erick, I'll be fucked. You need to help me hide this cunt and we'll say he fucked off out for a run.

Me: Lar, boy, this is fucked man we have to ring the shades. You can plead that the weed made you proper insane boy, you'll be alright.

Lar: Fuck no man. If you ring the shades, I'll just say it was fucking you who done it. 50-50 chance they'll believe me. HAHA fuck you, boy.

Fucking Lar. Just after killing a good friend of ours and he was trying to frame me for it already. I stood up, the adrenaline was coursing through me now, and for a minute I understood why it was so easy for him to kill Mayo. I grabbed his right hand with my left, to stop him swinging the cutter at me and gave him a swift puck to the side of his head with my right. Lar, the fat fuck, went down like a sack of golden wonders. Luckily for him, the leather of the couch was soft and worn so when his head impacted it, there wasn't much damage done.

I was sick of the fucker. I was sick of his attitude. I was sick of the fact that he thought he'd a divine right to the Titanic. I never got over the fact that'd he'd shifted my ol' doll and now he was after murdering Mayo over a piece of pizza. I climbed on top of the fella, put both my hands around his neck and started squeezing. Lar was much smaller than me. To be fair, he put up a bit of a struggle, but he was dead within a few minutes. I felt a bit better than his neck had snapped under my weight, rather than him suffocating to death. Suffocation would have been an awful way to go. I rolled off him onto the floor, absolutely exhausted. The house was in shit. Mayo's blood was all over the gaf. I looked around at what had happened. It hadn't registered with me yet that I'd just murdered one of my good friends. He annoyed the fuck outta me, but I'd known Lar since 1st year of secondary school. Sometimes I wanted him dead, but I never wanted to be the one to off him. It was all down to the madness that develops when a young Irish fella tries to do dry January. This madness had been triggered by our collective lust for a small, stupid piece of Italian bread, and it resulted in two of the boys being dead, and me being the one, surviving, murderous, sober cunt. I reached into the pizza box and found the Titanic. There was a small bit of blood on it, nothing you wouldn't be able to ignore. I just held it in my hand and stared at it. The longer I stared the funnier the whole situation became. Soon, I was laughing hysterically at the whole thing.

Carpet came in 20 minutes later with his date and found me, sitting in a pool of Mayo's blood next to Lar's lifeless corpse, howling laughing at the small slice of pizza in my hands. He tried to shake me out of it but couldn't so he rang the fucking shades. I didn't realise that though. All I could think of was how underrated Cumberland Sausage is on a pizza.

Kilogram Faeries

"Pure shreds bro, push day got me all types of swole.
Absolutely loving this new gym gear too bro, abso
comfort #irishfitfam #fitfam #protein #swole #follow-
forfollow #shredz #sikunt #shredded #irishbeef"

Kilo finished off his latest Insta caption and sent it off. It had 20 likes in the first 6 seconds. Pure viral, bro. He didn't mind all the dirty looks people gave him in the changing room for taking a topless picture in the mirror. They only hated him because he was so jacked. They didn't even comprehend what bulking season really was, and they couldn't cut for shit.

167 likes. Sick bro. Kilo lashed a heap of Whey protein into his mixer and shook it up. Peaches and cream flavour, abso delish. His real name was Eoin King. He'd gotten the nickname 'Kilo' because of a rumour going around UCC saying that he'd done a kilo of coke in one night and didn't fucking collapse and die. It hadn't happened at all but Eoin never bothered to correct anyone. It was sick story, bro. Plus, it gave him the chance to have his Insta username changed to '@Kilo_Gram', and there was no way he'd pass up on such a sweet opp. No way, man. Kilo did nutrition in UCC but he was from Meath, originally. He wanted to go to Trinity but didn't get the points in the Leaving, sickener. He

was defo the smartest bro in Clongos that year but he was absolutely positive Mr. Gallagher had paid off someone in the Department to make sure he failed geography. Gallagher had always been jealous of Kilo's legit shreds, and Kilo was convinced. The joke was on Gallagher now, there's no way he was getting 300 plus likes on any Insta post.

Kilo was due to graduate the following October of 2011, but he still didn't know what he was going to do. Like, obviously it's absolutely whopper to get that many likes on any post, and girls absolutely gushed for him but like, you couldn't get paid to post on Insta? That was the dream for sure man, but there was no way. Kilo was banking on getting a graduate-entry job in his dad's accountancy firm. He could totally breeze in there and concentrate on the more important things in life; insane gains and keeping the tan abso fresh. If there was one thing the man knew how to do, it was to sculpt the perfect physique, and make sure everyone knew about it. His self-marketing is straight-bodacious, bro. Kilo had like 2,000 followers on Instagram and they were all basically getting professional work outs plans from Kilo. After every topless post he'd put his work-out from that day right there in the comments, sans-charge. People were always calling Kilo vain and narcissistic but the bro was giving people sick workouts for free. That's a legit bro if you ask me.

Kilo was always talking about how he wished he'd be able to make money off of his 'totally bitchin'' insta page. We all thought he was insane. There was no way any of us thought you could make money from your social media page, not in 2011 anyway. It was unheard of. Some of the boys were still on Bebo like, there was no place for social media in the monetary world. Kilo was a visionary though, well he thought he was, anyway. He tried for months to come up with a way to make a job out of his insta. He got deactivated for awhile because he started charging girls in his DMs in return for topless pics of himself. For an extra tenner they could also claim to their friends he was their boyfriend. The poor bro only made 15 quid before he got shut down by the lads in Instagram's Admin department.

To say Kilo was spiralling that last semester of his final year is an understatement. Here he was, with a totally incredible social media profile, yet all the likes in the world couldn't make him any money. At this point he'd post a blurry picture of his protein shake with no caption and get 900 likes. There was no insta page like his back then. The man was losing his mind for sure. There was one time in March, myself and Kilo were going to go hit the muscle factory before a whopper night out so I called over to his gaff on College Road. I was already pumped to tear a hole in this chest sesh, you know? Anyway, I get to the house and the walls are legit covered in these 'algorithms' for how to convert likes into euros. It's important to understand that for all his marketing genius, Kilo did not understand the fundamental rules of simple mathematics. None of his equations made any sense. At the centre of it all was a massive scribing of an equation that simply read '1 like = €2' with no explanation whatsoever of how Kilo had come to this conclusion. I found Kilo, manically pouring strawberry whey protein into an already full shaker in the kitchen, as he repeated the words "Monetary gains, bro" over and over again. I'm not sure he'd even noticed that I was in the house. I left almost immediately after that. Kilo had proper freaked me out, so I had to move to Defcon 8 straight away no questions asked; I called his mother and told her Kilo had lost his mind.

It only took Kilo's old laid like 20 minutes to convince him to come home for a few days. It was study month anyway, so he didn't have any college work to be doing. Plus, the house in Meath had a sick home-gym so Kilo could get his work-outs done there no problem. I felt real bad about calling Kilo's own mother into the situation, but in my defence, the guy was clearly having a mental breakdown. He was a month away from finishing his undergrad and becoming a real adult, yet here he was obsessing over getting paid for his Instagram. A few days at home in the soft countryside of Meath would do him well. Plus, his mother was a serious hippy-liberal type. She was completely into all this alternate medicines like homeopathy and reiki, so she got Kilo on the water with like a pinch of cinnamon or whatever they use in it. Hydration is key for any serious gym-goer anyway so if nothing else, Kilo's mom was doing him a favour in that regard. Kilo's old laid was always harrowing on about New grange and faeries as well, about how the faeries had helped her to heal people in the past. I'd heard of people talk about angels in that way before, which is crazy enough in itself, but the idea of faeries healing people was on another level altogether. It's probably the sole reason Kilo's mom had decided to settle in Meath, just to be near the mystical lands of the faeries and New grange. The woman was tapped.

It's no understatement when I say that the three days Kilo spent at home in Meath changed the course of his entire life. I'd hardly believe what happened to be true if the results weren't so glaringly obvious and severe. It was a Wednesday, Kilo had just crushed a shoulder sesh in his home gym, uploaded five new posts on the gram, and taken his half bucket of essential supplements to get the gains in the right places; basic stuff. After his initial recovery from his work-out, Kilo's mom told him he'd to go for a walk to let the 'country of Ireland heal his body'. Kilo had known his mother for his whole life by now, and he knew not to question her beliefs. One time he made the mistake of implying the events of Harry Potter were fictitious, which resulted in his mom setting fire to his incredible collection of seasonal-Ibiza snapbacks. He hadn't made that mistake again since.

Kilo headed out for his walk as commanded. It was a dry March evening, fairly warm, so he decided to roll out in a fresh sleeveless-beater with the words 'Gains Ovr Brains' spread across the nipples. He did this just in case he came across a little cutie on his walk. As you'd expect, Kilo's mom lived as near to New grange as she could afford, due to her unyielding obsession with faeries, and myths about Cúchullann and those lads. In terms of places to go for walks, there were few places in the country with as nice scenery on offer. Kilo walked, earphones in for about half an hour. The watery-medicine-potion his mother had given him had filled his bladder to the brim by this point, and he was bursting to drain himself. He'd been walking on a quiet road but he didn't want to risk any of his surrounding neighbours seeing his lad and posting it on the Gram, so he nipped off into the wooded area that bordered the roads in Meath.

He walked until he couldn't see the road from the treeline any more. He found an open area, which was almost a perfect circle, with one mid-sized tree centred in the middle of it. It was as if the woods had made a natural urinal for walkers to unload their various bodily fluids on. He pulled down his skinny-jean joggers and let flow, which was met with the familiar, euphoric relief that comes with the release of urine that has been festering in the bladder for just that bit too long. As he stood there, lad in hand, he suddenly heard a soft giggle, accompanied by the sound of a bird's wings when the creature tried to hover in the one place. Forced, effortful beating of tiny wings. You'd have heard this sound if you've ever had a stupid fucker of a bird fly into your house, and panic around the place trying to escape again. Kilo quickly concealed his mick as his cheeks turned crimson red.

Kilo: Who's there?

Mystery voice: Tis only me ya gowl.

The reply had come from the other side of the tree. Kilo peered around and saw the being that the voice had come from. Kilo told me the description of this fella about 1000 times so I know it very well at this stage. This thing looked like a miniature version of a middle-aged balding ol' fella. The type you'd see down at the pub at like 2pm on a Thursday slurping pints. He was overweight with a mystical, white 5 o'clock shadow on his face. He wasn't miniature the same way a dwarf is, but rather just a smaller version of a regularly proportioned human. He was just about 4 foot, Kilo said. He also had these comically tiny wings on him, which were more for show than anything. They flapped, apparently autonomously, but were in absolutely no way capable of lifting this fat, smelly creature off the floor. This thing was wearing a tattered burgundy, corduroy suit, with an egg-white shirt underneath. His pathetic, little wings protruded from a half-hearted whole in the back of his jacket. He was leaning against the old, tree, stealing sips from a poorly rolled cigarette in his left hand. His breath sounded the way broke glass does when you stand on it, all crackly and sore.

Kilo: What the fuck are you, bro?

Chuck: The name's Chuck, you fucking douche. I'm one of the faeries that works over at the Hill of Tara. You've some langer on you, fella.

Kilo had always been proud of the dimensions of the weapon genetics had bestowed upon him. He'd never seen his old fella's, but he imagined that the man had a similar one on him.

Kilo: You're a faery? Jesus, my nutbag of a mother was actually right, that's gas. Why are you in the woods trying to watch fellas piss?

The faery had a fed-up look on his face. Chuck had been dealing with people for more than half millennia, yet he always wondered why he had to entertain the thick stupid ones. Assignments were given based on performance and Chuck had a rich history of not giving a fuck about the outcomes of his. The bureau had been trying to push him out for centuries.

Chuck: I don't hang around here waiting for lads like you to whip out your langer for a slash. This is my jurisdiction; my tree. You're more or less after pissing on my office you complete and utter tool.

Kilo: Gosh, bro. You're a dick! I thought faeries were supposed to be sound.

Chuck: C'm'ere fella, I was about to help you out with your career problems but to be honest you're more of a douche than I realized so you can jog on, hai.

Chuck began to turn away from Kilo, pulling on his rollie as he moved. Kilo perked up at the sound of this. He was in the middle of the woods in Meath, talking to a fat faery named Chuck, and now it appeared the thing that was causing him severe mental anguish could be figured out.

Kilo: Whoa, you can help me make money from the gram? That would be totally legitimised, bro.

Chuck: Kilo I'm a fucking faery I could solve this in a matter of minutes, you uneducated little prick. Let's say I can make it so that you can make money from your Instagram posts. I can make it so you get free accommodation, food, anything at all, once you promise the business some 'exposure' on your social media feeds. It'll also be the case that people will start paying you for your work-out plans, club appearances, all of that. You won't be world-famous, but people will reluctantly know who you are, and you'll never have to do a real day's work for your entire life

Kilo: No fucking way, bro? Are you for real? That would be the abso dream, man, for reals.

Chuck: I can make all of that happen. But there is one condition. It's pretty small and I doubt it'll ever come up but these things only get approved if you take on some sort of risk. Basically, any time a radio station refers to you as an 'influencer' I'm afraid you'll lose a centimetre off of that hefty langer of yours. Look, it's not much of a risk, what are the chances of that happening?

Kilo: Bro, I could give away two inches of this thing and still be a total monster. Besides, does anyone even know the word 'influencer'? I don't think so, dude. I'm gonna be set for life, bro let's make it happen.

Chuck: Grand job, lad. It'll probably take 24 hours or so to push through so I'd imagine this will start taking effect there at some stage tomorrow. Fair fucks to ya, man. G'luck.

You'd imagine an ancient being like himself would have just disappeared into thin air. Instead he uncovered his push scooter from a near-by bushling, and began slowly, awkwardly making his way along the uneven terrain in the opposite direction that Kilo had come from. Kilo more or less skipped the whole way home. Either he was tripping balls, or some insane Celtic magic lark, had just occurred. Whichever it was, tomorrow would reveal all.

Seven years later

Kilo rolled over. The taste of 3am shots of sambuca lashed the inside of his dry mouth. His head felt like a feminist Hen Party; absolutely no-craic. He'd slept alone, again, and had drank himself into oblivion, again. He lazily picked up his phone, to check the time. He had an unimaginable number of notifications, both from his Instagram page, and from LGBT Ireland. His most recent insta-pick, a blurry, angled shot of his bare ass, had surpassed 8,000 likes already. It was 8:03am. He fumbled in the dusky, morning light for the bottle of Southern Comfort he kept near-by. Two swigs for the boys in green. Every morning had started this way for the last 2 and a half years. Every morning had started this way since he lost what could be considered a recognisable penis. All that remained was a small skin-tag and a pair of hairy, floppy balls. He'd gone back to the opening in the woods of Meath with a gun the odd time when he was off his mind to try to kill the faery that had forsaken him. The lads, fuck the whole world thought he was insane. Blaming the loss of his 'colossal langer' on the magic of some smelly, imaginary faery. In fairness, the first year or so of the covenant were good to Kilo. He made a killing from his work-outs and club appearances, and could get free munch everywhere. It wasn't 'til the summer of 2012 that more of his kind started coming out of the woodworks and the label 'Influencer' became a reality. Kilo was fucked after that. Initially, he didn't really notice the change in length. As the months went on though, his shaft became smaller, and smaller, the more popularity he won. It tore him apart, literally and figuratively. He had the exact fame and career he'd always wanted, yet he had no penis to enjoy it with.

The media became obsessed with Kilo's personal life, and why he was literally never seen with a woman, or man, *ever*. By the end of the 2013, Kilo couldn't hack the attention so he came out as 'genderless, non-gender-conforming'. The first of his kind. The backlash of this was a renewed surge of popularity, especially amongst the LGBT community. He was an icon, the first non-gender conforming man of his time. By then he had no penis whatsoever, and his public image had become something of a world-wide phenomenon. I suppose you could say he peaked in 2014. He received a load of awards in the New Year, but his proudest moment was representing Austria in the Eurovision Song Contest in the Summer of 2014, and winning the whole thing, under the name of Conchita. We all knew it was him though and the whole event was bodacious, classic Kilo move.

I don't really see Kilo too often anymore, he's rarely here in Ireland, too famous for that now. But yeah, that's why I have this tattoo 'Kilo-Gram' on my bicep, to commemorate one bro's life-time achievement, plus I'm LITERALLY always in the gym. Anyway do you have snapchat? Abso hate texting people on Tinder, lol.

The Lobster Clause

When you order lobster in a restaurant, and I mean the full lobster not just lobster claws, they boil the poor things alive to cook them. It has something to do with food poisoning. Apparently a dead lobster gets infested fairly quickly with bacteria that are not good for humans whatsoever. Did you know all that? I did. It's actually the reason that, when I started killing people, I decided to boil them alive. If it's humane enough for lobsters, it's humane enough for humans. I've only killed 93 people though, and all of them deserved it.

You'd think that by now I would have been caught. I mean, I know I'm a sociopath or whatever, and I'm quite intelligent, but I don't overexert myself when it comes to covering my tracks. I did in the beginning of course, but as it became easier and more routine, I became less careful. Now, 93 kills deeps, it almost feels like I'll never be caught, and that's half the fun. I think there's an unwritten code amongst serial killers. On some level we all desire to be caught, eventually. We crave that notoriety, the infamy. Of course, you can't be caught too earlier, because then people think you're a sloppy murderer; a once-off. You have to have a good number of kills under your belt to be given a calling card, to be identified as a serial killer. Have you ever smelled boiling human flesh by the way? It kind of smells how tires do when the rubber is burning into tarmac, mixed with rotten egg whites. I suppose we're predisposed to be disgusted by the smell of burning or boiling human flesh. I imagine lobsters are disgusted by the smell of other burning lobsters, if they can smell that sort of thing.

Anyway, the smell kind of grows on you after a while. It kind of stains your clothes too, the same way it's almost impossible to get skunk spray out of your skin. It was hard to explain the bang off me initially to my family, considering I work in an insurance office down town. They seem to have bought the story that I drive passed the tire place on the way home, and when the traffic is bad I'm stuck outside it for ages, so the smell of melting rubber gets in my hair. How on earth they bought that is beyond me. Honestly, non-sociopaths are fucking morons most of the time, so naïve, so willing to believe in the best of people. I made my cover story lazy on purpose, just so that thrill of being caught might drift back into my experiential zone. But they just accepted it, with minimal resistance. See I don't have any remorse for my killings. To be quite frank, I'm proud of all the terrible lives I've ended. The thing is, I've gotten kinda bored with it all. The smell of boiling flesh no longer exhilarates me. The spike of adrenaline I used to get when I first abducted my newest victim isn't as exaggerated, or euphoric. I've gotten to a point in all this where it's starting to feel like a job rather than a labour of love. I no longer love doing all of this. I'm doing because I'm waiting to be caught, I'm waiting to become the notorious 'Lobster-Maker'. It almost seems as though nobody has noticed all these disappearances. Maybe the people I've killed are really scumbags after all. Maybe I'm like the character Denzel plays in that Equalizer movie. I'm killing, but maybe it's for the greater good? Still, I want the notoriety. I want to be feared and hated because that type of fame lasts. Nobody remembers the good guy, but the villain is always remembered in the history book.

Because of all this, because I'm bored, I decided to devise a scheme to get myself caught. I made that sound as if this would be in any way difficult. Basically, I just let one of my would-be victims get away, and I let him see my face as well. His name is Martin Fencing. He's the owner of a restaurant called 'The Lobster Clause' in town. He's a monster for his unique selling point alone. Basically, with every order, whether you order lobster or not, they still boil a lobster for eating. If you order it, it's yours, if not, they feed the stray cats out the back, this freshly boiled lobster. This idea is the name sake of the restaurant, and it's a pretty successful attempt at getting more people to order lobster. This lobster clause is the reason I wanted to kill Martin, but now it'll be a prominent factor in my court trial, and will hopefully earn me the nickname that I rightfully deserve. All I did was loosely tie the bonds around Martin's hands so that, whilst I was preparing his tankard with water, he would notice these poorly constructed bonds and free himself. To make it convincing I, of course, gave chase and almost caught him too. Martin isn't in good shape by any stretch, so faking that he was even able to get away from me was difficult. Eventually, I let Martin get away. He found his way out of the warehouse I had brought him to and escaped into the night. That night brought with it an air of relief. My killing spree, of 93 lives across 2 years had finally come to an end. I would be tried and charged, spend the remainder of my life in prison, but my legacy would be cemented.

The police never came. I stayed in that warehouse all night and they never showed. I expected Martin to go straight to them, to tell them of my location and what I was planning to do to him. I even stayed until lunchtime the next day. Nobody turned up. I'd the radio on and there wasn't even a news bulletin about Martin's escape from my clutches. I was furious. Had it been that uninteresting, that atraumatic an experience, that Martin hadn't even written it off as memorable? I had made it crystal clear that I'd intended to murder him, and he had apparently shrugged it off as another run-of-the-mill Tuesday. How often did this weirdo get abducted? The idea that Martin Fencing hadn't taken me serious was unbearable. I should have boiled him, like all the others. I should have just done it. I picked up my phone, and was about to smash it off a near-by wall when it began to ring, vibrating loudly.

Me: Err, hello?

Voice: Is this Ernie Ward??

The voice on the other end of the phone was equal parts formal and clinical.

Me: Yes, speaking.

Voice: Mr. Ward, this is Federal Agent Sean Purney. We have just received an anonymous tip of your whereabouts and of your, let's say hobby, over the last 2 years. This tip was accompanied with visual evidence of your side venture. The building you currently occupy is surrounded by field agents. You can either come quietly, or I can give my men the order to shoot on sight.

Me: No, no need for haste Agent Purney, I'll come quietly.

Purney: A wise decision, Mr. Ward. There's a town car outside the front of the building. You best be unarmed.

This was the weirdest arrest ever. At least I thought it was. Maybe the drama of arrests on TV just isn't how it plays out in the real word. I was expecting a raid, and cameras, and frankly, more excitement. Although the arrest of the infamous *Lobster Maker* was anti-climactic, I was sure my trial would be one for the books. I took the stairs down from the second floor. It was dark outside, and it was beginning to mist. The evaporation fell like sweat in a steam room. I peered out the window of the front door. There didn't seem to be anyone in sight. I could see the town-car outside, its engine turning over impatiently. I pushed open the door and stepped out into the night. My first step was followed by some urgent shuffling. A hand with a cloth smothered my mouth and nose, another hand grasped across my chest in an attempt to sub-miss my arms. I knew the smell straight away. I used the stuff often enough to know it was too late to get away. Chloroform. This didn't feel very law-enforcement-ish. It felt more kidnap-y, more serial killer vibes. I was too excited about being caught to even consider anyone else would come here for me. I passed out just as they opened the door to the boot of the car.

I regained consciousness whilst still in the confined space. The engine churned on as the car rolled along slowly, but steady. There were slithers of light squeezing through the edge of the boot's door, too dim to illuminate the inside, but bright enough to trace out the edges of the boot. I had no idea whether this was the police or some fanatic. It definitely didn't feel very legal, and so I concluded that the cops being involved was quite unlikely. The car's brakes engaged suddenly and my full weight was flung against the back of the seats in the rear of the car. A dagger of pain across my forehead was confirmation that I was indeed still very much in the boot. We had stopped, and I heard two car doors opening and closing quite uniformly. Crunching footsteps indicated that one of the people who had exited the car was on his way to the rear, presumably to open the boot. The locking mechanism clicked as it unlocked and the door of the boot swung open. A fat, grumpy-faced man with pungent BO looked down at me menacingly. He looked like a Leonard, so I made a mental note to refer to him as such. Perhaps I'd get the chance to call him 'Big L', I wasn't really sure where the evening was going yet.

Big Leonard grabbed me by the hair and dragged me from the boot of the car. This was a terrible first impression and made me dislike Leonard very much. I imagined he was also the man who had chloroformed me quite recently. He obviously had an aptitude for the grunt work, as I could not imagine this hefty man was the brains of any operation.

Leonard continued to hold me by the hair as he dragged me from the car to the back-alley door of some vaguely familiar building. It was more the deserted alleyway that was familiar, rather than the building, but I had definitely been here before. We turned left immediately once inside, and Big L lugged me into a dark, empty room with one chair in the middle under a single, hanging lightbulb. It was extremely cliché as an interrogation scene, and I questioned again whether this was actually the melodrama of the cops. Leonard cable-tied me to the chair without a word, breathing heavily as he did so. I could feel his unhealthy wheeze on my neck and decided that I very much wanted to kill him. Leonard left the room and locked the door behind him. I was alone.

It must have been 50 minutes before he decided to come in. He stood by the door initially, far enough away so that I couldn't make out his face in the shadows, yet close enough that I could smell him. The smell of death. The same type of smell you'd feel drifting through the air on a Sunday morning walking through the markets. The smell of fresh fish bounced from him to my nostrils in nauseating waves. He stepped forward into the light, his creepy pedo-moustache stretched across the edge of his lip. His tongue darted in and out of his mouth, trying to keep the rim of his orifice moist. Martin. Fucking. Fencing. The building must have seemed familiar because it was the back entrance to The Lobster Clause.

Martin: You know, I wasn't sure if the stories were true. A man, boiling people alive because he hated animal cruelty. But here you are.

Me: Here I am.

Martin: I was a bit disappointed though. You're very sloppy, leaving me get away and all.

Me: by design, you melon. I wanna be caught, to secure my legacy as the Lobster Maker.

Martin: You wanted to be caught.... By the police?

Me: Well, yeah.

Martin: (laughs) and you understand I'm not the police?

Me: …

Martin: Sir, I don't know who you are, and by the end of tonight, nobody else will either. This series of boiling people will go down as, quite frankly, a disturbing unsolved killing spree. The best part of it is, you'll just be pasted as yet another victim of this madness!

The current situation slowly dawned on me. Martin had escaped, and immediately surmised a plan to recapture me, and take justice into his own hands. If I didn't make it out of there alive, all my work would have been in vain, and I'd never get the infamy I had earned.

Martin Fencing slithered toward the wall and flicked a light-switch to the right of the door he had entered the room from. The house lights came on, causing me to squint as the harsh white illuminated the room. As my eyes adjusted, the full weight of the situation came crashing down. To the left, there was a 15-foot water tank. The tank was occupied by around 20 large, deep-water lobsters. It was hard to say exactly how many, as they clambered over each other in the swirling water of the tankard. Martin walked to a control panel besides the tank and adjusted a few settings. For a few minutes nothing happened. Martin stood there awkwardly, almost waiting for something to happen.

As sure as a watched kettle doesn't boil, it appears that a watched tankard of lobsters takes an age to heat up. After 10 minutes steam started rising from the surface of the water. Martin figured that he probably should have switched on the tank 20 minutes before he revealed himself, to continue the dramatic effect. It didn't matter now, anyway; the show was beginning. It didn't take long for the water to start bubbling, and for the live lobsters to start squirming as the temperature became more unbearable. As the lobsters squirmed, so did I. *The bastard,* I thought. *Torturing me by making me watches the animals I love boil to death!*

• • •

Martin smiled as he watched Ward's distressed attempts to break free from his chair. This man had taken more than enough friends from this life. He had even tried to kill Martin himself. This man deserved everything coming to him. He watched as Leonard lumbered up behind Ward's chair and lift it from beneath with relative ease. He was fat, but he was strong-fat. He watched as Ernie Ward squirmed in terror on the seat, surely realizing what was happening. The tank had now come to a full boil, hot water spewing from the lips of the top of the tank. The lobsters were all but dead now, currently cooking inside the boiling environment. Leonard walked backwards up the mobile-steps next to the tank, dragging the chair up behind him. As he reached the landing, he took a moment to breathe, squatted low, and pushed the chair up to meet his chin's level. He used this momentum to swing the chair, and its passenger over the lip of the tank and down into the water. There were agonising screams instantly.

• • •

Being boiled alive is, without question, the worst experience I had ever imagined. It's the reason I had chosen to boil people in the first place, to ensure their suffering. Waves of unbearable heat, constantly rippling across the skin's surface, causing it the melt and tear, was not something one found bearable. Death didn't take long. You technically never boil to death, you drown. The boiling merely adds relentless pain whilst your body drowns in the process. My final thoughts were of my legacy, and how nobody would ever know that I had been the notorious Lobster-Maker. Martin Fencing had ensured that much. My mind settled briefly on the fat-oaf who had thrown me into the tank, just before I died. I never learned his real name, and I hoped to fuck it was Leonard, that'd be gas enough.

Blinding Clarity

There is no conclusive evidence that Gandhi ever said the phrase '*an eye for an eye will make the whole world blind*'. He may have said it, he may not have. The world kind of just accepted it as fact. On another note, William Shakespeare actually wrote once that '*The eyes are the windows to the soul.*' Two famous men, two famous quotes, highlighting the effect the eyes have. They're important. It's how most of us take first impressions. In a simple blink, we weigh up an entire person's worth based solely on their appearance. This is the sole premise with which dating apps such as Tinder and Bumble were built upon. Our eyes dictate our vanity, how superficial we are. They possess our power to judge. This was a fact Aidan Cooper learned at 23 years old.

Aidan was a millennial. If you don't know that word, it means he was born at some time in the decades surrounding the millennia. In Aidan's case it was the decade previous, in the year 1995. Aidan was 23. Like many millennials, Aidan was pathologically self-obsessed. The generation he belonged to had normalised narcissism, prioritising how life looked, rather than how life was. His life revolved meticulously around his social media profiles, with most of his time being spent on displaying how unbelievably perfect his life was. Aidan was unaware of the damage being done to

his psychological health, as most of his peers were. He believed that his life on Instagram was a true reflection of his
real life, and he also believed this to be true for everyone
else. This is not to say that the fault belonged to Aidan. He
was merely a product of social conditioning and a lack of
awareness. He was just another cog in a distorted system, a
blip that would have gone unremarkable and unnoteworthy
had the events of the September 3rd, 2018 not happened.
You see, on September 3rd, 2018 Aidan Cooper permanent-
ly and definitively lost his eyesight.

There was a car crash. Plenty of serious injuries, but none
dead. The incident kind of reminds me of how Daredevil
gets his powers, but nobody got powers in this story. It was
just tragedy and pain. Aidan was in the passenger seat of his
mother's car at the time. She lost most of her right leg, the
surgeons couldn't salvage it. Dozens of tiny shards of glass
entered Aidan's eyes in the aftermath. The engine of the
Arctic that had collided with them exploded a few moments
after contact, causing the windows of their Toyota to ex-
plode. The shards were too many and too small to feasibly
extract and save Aidan's eyesight. Both eyes were removed.
Two new glass eyes were inserted for the sake of aesthetics,
but Aidan would rarely remove the sunglasses that would
soon be etched into his identity. Everything changed that
day.

The support Aidan received was phenomenal. Floods of
well-wishers submerged his timelines, his personal social
media feeds. As he sat there on that first day in his intimate
darkness, he heard his phone seizure frantically on the table
as new messaged vibrated in. His mother periodically hob-
bled in on her one and a bit legs, and read a string of mes-
sages to him, but there were too many to get through them
all. All this love, real or otherwise, sent directly to Aidan's
phone. But now, somehow it didn't mean as much. Aidan
couldn't experience it first hand, and so it really didn't con-
nect or hammer home. No amounts of likes or tweets would

bring back his vision. No amount of new followers could soften the impact of a life-changing accident. Suddenly, Instagram could no longer provide the artificial self-esteem that had substituted self-love for so long. Suddenly Aidan had no likes, had no followers, or any of the dopamine that came with such things. In those first weeks of coming to terms with his new reality, Aidan began his first battle with very real and very harsh depression. He ordered his mother to delete his social media accounts and replaced his high level of self-esteem with a high level of self-pity.

The weeks rolled on. If you can imagine, the trials of learning to live without eyesight are almost insurmountable, and this becomes even more of a struggle when your will to even live is also diminishing. Lost in relentless darkness, Aidan refused to learn any new skills to help his situation. He scoffed at brail, arguing that brail wouldn't enable him to use his phone, the only thing he believed was worth reading anything from. He declined any offers from friends to visit, arguing that he didn't look anything like the fella he was before and was essentially no longer Aidan. He hated the idea of being pitied or looked down upon. He was furious about everything, about how he couldn't even tell if he was dressed well, or if his hair was done properly. All the superficial things that were so key to Aidan's life were now out of his control, and so Aidan felt like nothing was worthwhile anymore, now that he couldn't be seen.

As time trickled by Aidan slowly began to grow accustomed to his new existence. With each day his other senses heightened and became a more reliable resource for navigating through the dark. He started leaving the house more often, taking pride in his ability to get to and from, unassisted. He still ached for the technology which once made him feel truly connected to the world. For a brief period, he resorted to using the voice generation software on his phone to read out what would appear on his timelines. Unfortunately, the technology was nowhere near intuitive enough to adhere to the needs of a blind Aidan, as it failed to ignore irrelevant and unimportant details. It also struggled with his inconsistent Southern Irish accent and often got even the simplest of commands completely backward. Using the basic-bitch A.I. was almost more frustrating than having no access to social media, and this period of potential adaptation ceased quickly.

If you'd known Aidan before the accident, you'd have seen the true face of superficiality that exists in his generation. His opinions of most people were formed and cemented within the first few moments of seeing a person. Subconscious awareness of micro-gestures, dress sense, and body language, all played roles in this vague judgement. Aidan, for example, would decide you were 'gay' if you dressed and behaved a certain way, and even if you weren't, it just meant you weren't out yet. He decided whether you were cool, a lad, a bitch, a slut, a loser or a conceited douche all within the first few seconds of sharing the same space. This isn't some sort of super-power Aidan had, rather it was a common characteristic of his millennial-social media culture. Everything, in his world, was judged on perceived snapshots, rather than a wholesome example of what was real. You were ear-marked, categorised and labelled long before any underlying personality presented itself. This doesn't necessarily mean that these snap-judgments were accurate, far from it actually. However, they were considered to be useful to maintain social hierarchies and the status quo, meaning they were taken very seriously. Influencers were those who learned to prosper in such a system, taking advantage of vanity and unstable self-esteem patterns to gain popularity. Aidan wasn't one of these true influencer types though. He had thousands of followers, yes, but he was more of just an out-going popular 'lad', making his name by being rigidly straight and masculine. He was a lad, driven by ego and terrified of any semi-feminine thing that may bring his own masculinity into question.

Why is any of that relevant? Well, as Aidan's memory of having eyesight faded, so too did his instinct to make snap judgements. Since he could no longer actually see people, he couldn't judge anyone by what they looked like, or wore. He could no longer group people based on looks and perceived status, nor could he group himself in this way. Instead, Aidan could only know people by how they talked to him and to each other. People who would have never been within Aidan's circle before the accident now frequently spent time with him. Without the filters of judgement, Aidan found most people to be pleasant, insightful and enjoyable. What's more, is that he began to find his old social circles intolerable. Without eyesight, the unmasked narcissistic, and undeveloped personalities soaked through like spilt milk on a carpet.

I'd like to be able to say here that Aidan was a completely changed person, but it's not the case. That type of dramatic transformation only happens in movies. He still held the arrogant swagger he always had and was still irrefutably occupied with gaining his eyesight back, and figuring out how to get his social status reinstated. At least that's what he'd have you believe. Aidan had changed in many other ways. He no longer judged people based on superficial values. He went weeks at a time without even mentioning social media, sometimes even longer. He had become a far better listener and by association, a much better friend and person. Whether Aidan was aware of it or not, he was much happier, and a far better person blind, than he ever had been with perfect vision. Social anxiety doesn't exist without vision, and so without the pressures of being 'seen' Aidan had found a way to be happy.

He'd never admit it out loud, but Aidan often noted quietly to himself, how blessed he was to have been in that car crash.

Born-Again Virgin

The average person in Ireland loses their virginity straight out of the statutory gate, at age 17. That's your bang-average person. Some go a little younger, some older. The fellas tend to lose it a bit younger because, quite frankly, they're pure horny. They don't think about the meaning of losing one's virginity as much as girls do, but that's more of a blood circulation issue than an intellect problem. Anyway, most people lose their virginity in and around 17. Not our Denny though. Denny lost his V-card at the ripe age of 12 years old.

On the surface, it's very much one of those situations where a young fella says he rode the babysitter when he was like 10. Everyone laughs and nobody believes him. Denny tells his fair share of whoppers as well, so the suspect fits the crime. However, I can report on this occasion, the young fella did actually ride the babysitter when he was 12, not 10. Her name won't be disclosed due to risk of defamation. After all, she was 15, 3 years older than Denny-boy. On top of that, whereas Denny would have been seen as a 'legend' if anyone believed him, this poor girl would have been ridiculed and shamed as a 'slut'. Not exactly fair if you ask me, but there are double standards, and life is certainly not fair.

Now I won't get into the fine details here, mainly due to the legality of it all. The take-home message is that Denny lost his virginity at age 12. He wouldn't have sex again until he was 18, and was active semi-often until he was 22. That's when things took a turn south for Den, and that's where our story really begins.

Denny celebrated his 25th birthday in late January, with his parents and a few close friends. He had to start shift the next morning, so it consisted of cake and a few bottles of beer. Nothing too wild. Like all birthdays do, the day forced Denny to recant the story of his life so far. He missed the glory days of college, which now felt like a lifetime ago. Denny had peaked socially just after secondary school, and it had been a gradual decline ever since. He didn't really see the fruits of this decline until later, but it was glaringly obvious now on his 25th birthday. See, for all his early success in the sexual domain, from the early loss of virginity to the frequent activity in his first few years of adulthood, Denny hadn't had sex, or even been looked at by a woman in over 2 years. The last time Denny had sex was the night he graduated from his degree in BIS from UCC. He had drunk and disappointing sex with one of the girls from his course. Ever since then, not due to lack of trying, Denny had not been able to get his hole in any shape or form.

It was one of those things that happens to a larger number of people than you'd think. It's actually surprising. The difficulty with it is, nobody that it happens to is ever willing to disclose this information, and so sexual drought of this length is an isolated problem, handled entirely by the individual. Although, unbeknownst to him, Denny had four other friends in his peer group who were experiencing a similar drought. Denny had to navigate this embarrassing ordeal in solo mode.

Ending a sexual drought is trickier than one would think. Of course, there's the option of paying for intimacy, but this doesn't exactly feel earned. Similar to buying Instagram followers, whilst nobody else will really know the truth, you'll always feel as though you've cheated yourself. Therefore, to truly end a drought, an authentic experience must be acquired. The difficulty with pulling during a drought lies in the production of desperation pheromones. Members of the opposite sex can subconsciously pick up on desperation stink, and find themselves inexplicably unattracted to you, no matter how charming or beautiful you may be. The second obstacle to ending a drought comes from the urgency of the situation. As you haven't had sex in so long, you can't afford to attract a partner, rather you must actively find one. This is different from the pheromone issue in that this factor affects both genders differently. Women tend to go for a man who isn't looking to pull them. A man who is aloof and distant, rather than the fella who follows them around all night, trying at every possible moment to strike up a conversation. We call this the Attractive Light Hypothesis. Simply put, moths, for example, are attracted to light when it is stationary and confident in its position, but will fly away from moving lights that chase them, such as headlights and torches. So although a sexual drought suggests an urgency to chase, most desirable partners are those who don't chase. What does all this mean for our Denny? Basically, it meant Denny was fucked (but not literally).

Unfortunately with a drought, the longer it was fixated on, the more severe it became. His desperation pheromone stench somehow extended through his phone as he couldn't even get a match on Tinder, let alone attract a woman in real life. The drought had been going on 2 years by his 25th birthday, but Denny wouldn't see any physical effects of this drought until 3 months later.

I don't really know how to explain this. It's something that you've probably joked about with your friends when they haven't pulled in a while. Personally, I thought it was just that; a joke or a myth. I know now that it's not. See, after 27 months of sexless existence, Denny's virginity grew back. I know what you're thinking, virginity isn't a physical thing that you lose, and I know. This is true the first time you have virginity, but Denny is the first case I know of where it's come back. The second time you become a virgin, there's a very marked physical attribute that comes with it.

Nothing new grows so to speak. It's important to note here too that I can't confirm what happens to a woman in this particular situation. I can confirm that what happens to a man *definitely* does not happen to women. Now, you're familiar with the term 'blue balls'. It's a colloquial term used to describe how a man hasn't been allowed to relieve his most primal urges. Basically, he hasn't shot his load in a while. Well, while this is a lovely metaphor for the fellow who hasn't gotten the job done in a week, this metaphor became a literal reality for Denny. His balls (and sack too) become a disturbingly smurfish hue of blue. Denny had literal blue balls, the brand of the 2nd time virgin.

There were already huge obstacles to ending a drought as we discussed. On top of those, Denny now had detestable blue testicles. If, on the off chance, Denny managed to convince a young woman to want to have sex with him, he'd still have to explain his bizarre blue scrotal sack. There was absolutely no way anyone could pull that off.

Now Denny's balls changed colour dramatically overnight, so as you can imagine the onset of panic was instant and heavy-handed. His mind instantly assumed it was some sort of STI, although he wondered how involuntary celibacy could land him with one. Too embarrassed to tell his family and friends, or even the family doctor, Denny booked an urgent appointment with a local sexual health clinic. There was, not surprisingly, no answer to be given there either. All blood tests and urine samples came back clean. The staff nurse even remarked that they were '*the cleanest samples she'd seen in decades.*' Denny was distraught as you can imagine. He was scared, both for his future, and literally afraid of his bright blue balls, which almost seemed to glow now. As he drove home from his follow-up appointment, the rain pelted down in the dark. The red brake lights of the cars in the rain were hypnotic and calming. Denny's mind searched far and wide for answers to his peculiar circumstance. Surely someone else had experienced this blue ball fiasco before. He cursed his lack of sexual activity. He cursed God for basically making him a virgin again. Cruel and merciless God.

It may have been the soothing ambiance of brake lights in the rain, or perhaps Denny's raw anger for God, but he suddenly knew exactly where to go. He suddenly realised that there were buildings full of perpetual virgins across the planet. Surely these sexless mongers would know exactly how to help Denny, outside the realm of medicine. Denny whipped a U-turn and headed directly for the nearest Catholic Church.

Denny had never been a huge fan of religion. He had nothing against the premise, it just never enticed him. The fact that church pews were so unnecessarily uncomfortable didn't help either. Coming to a church in the night, as the rain torrented down, created an eerie atmosphere. The wheels of his dinky Fiesta crunched to a halt on the gravel outside. Denny dashed through the downpour and pushed the creaky door of the church open with a decisive urgency. He was nervous, mainly because there was a high probability the priest on shift wouldn't have a clue what to say to him. There were a handful of devout lingering near the confession boxes. Denny took an awkward knee in the pews nearby and waited for his turn. He didn't have to wait long.

He shut the coffin-like door behind him and squeezed onto the small stool in the confessional. He could see the shadowed face of the priest behind the placard. "Tell me your sins, my child". The priest's voice had an air of routine boredom. Denny inhaled deeply and proceeded to tell this strange clergyman everything. He told him of the early loss of virginity. He went into unnecessary detail for each of his sexual encounters. The priest left out several gasps and grunts of disgust throughout. Denny revealed how he hadn't had sex in several years, and that now, his balls had turned a horrible blue colour. The priest had sat through this entire ordeal in disgust. However, he became alert and urgent at the mention of these mysterious blue testicles.

"Blue testicles you say??"

"Yes, Father."

"Show me them."

"What Father?!"

"Show me your balls, boy! There's no time!"

Denny was confused and very unsure, but he was desperate for answers, and it seemed this priest may have some. Denny dropped his trousers and revealed his blue genitalia. In this darkness of the confessional, it was clear that his balls were indeed glowing in an ultraviolet blue brilliance.

The Priest gasped, "You have been chosen!!"

He rushed out of his side of the confession box and pulled Denny out of his. By now the church was deserted. He yanked down his own garments to reveal his own pair of glowing balls hanging between his knees. "You are of the cloth, my boy! A born-again virgin!" Their balls glowed in unison, the light pulsating in the dimly lit church.

Two years later, the young Father Denny Foster delivered his first sermon.

Gut Feeling

Malevolence is the true default of human nature. Hard to admit that, it's even harder to fully appreciate what that means. We prefer to be bad and do bad things. Being good is abnormal. It's easy to explain why someone would murder, it's very difficult to unload why people don't. The same premise goes for life generally. Life is suffering. For the most part, life is pain and hardship and misfortune and bad timing and all the rest. There are only small blips of good dotted throughout which makes it all worthwhile. What I mean to say is, for life to be good, you must fully work for it. If you don't work for the good, then life quickly slips back into suffering, and so it's a constant effort. The Greeks knew this. The story of Sisyphus pushing a rock up a hill that he'll never summit illustrates this idea. The Old Testament has many tales of this idea too, most notably in Job, who maintains faith and work ethic throughout the many ordeals he is made to suffer. Life is suffering, and humans are mostly bad by default. Prometheus was said to have unleashed the contents of Pandoras' box onto humanity. Within the box were such things as famine, disease, war, and hope. You see, although life is suffering and terrible, humans endure it all, and deem it worthwhile due to hope. Hope is the instinctive idea that things will eventually get better, and it's the reason people have endured daily and terrible suffering for millennia. Bad things when happen when hope is lost.

Hope in its truest form saves lives. Hope is the base concept which inspires grit, resilience, the ability to toughen out the storm. Hope has ended wars, both in the physical world and the mental. Hope crumbles corruption, it insists on things being better. Hope is inherently good. Hope only goes bad when it disappears.

Every life is hopeful. Each life has potential or a chance for prosperity. Not all lives fulfil their hopeful potential, but every life does fulfil some sort of potential. As much as each life has a positive potential, they also have a negative potential. If you believe in destiny, then you might say that there's nothing you can do to change which path you walk down, it'll just happen, anyway. That might be true, we have no way of knowing. What we do know though, is that when a person loses hope, things can seem a lot worse than they might be.

Ethan's mother died when he was a young child. He could remember parts of it. His sister Lily couldn't remember anything she was a baby when it happened. Ethan remembered head scarfs, and medicine bottles, and reassuring voices. He remembered his mother's gentle smile and his father's whiskey. Eventually, the cancer killed her. Ethan remembered not understanding the full weight of it at the time. He remembered the suit his Aunt had got him, but the funeral itself was a fog. The most prominent memory from the weeks after that were more feelings than anything biographical. Ethan could remember knowing his dad was struggling.

The smell of stale whiskey on a person's breath isn't something any child should be familiar with. Nor should any child have to stand over his infant sister, to protect her from the onslaught of their drunken father. It wasn't Ethan's fault their dad was struggling, but it was definitely not Lily's.

Ethan was only 7 when the hitting began, and even though he was never strong enough to hold off his father's attacks, beating him was satisfying enough for Lily to avoid any damage. It seemed their lost father had some line that he wouldn't cross. The beatings were rare and infrequent, but they still happened. Ethan learned quickly that the faster he began to cry, the faster the beatings stopped. The years went by. Every time Ethan sensed a beating coming on, he made Lily hide in her room. She protested but did as she was told. They both knew what their father could be capable of. The beatings stopped when Ethan was 15 when Lily was 10. They stopped when their father was found hanging in his room by his belt.

Fortunately, neither Ethan nor Lily found him. Their Aunt did. There was a note, outlining how life had been meaningless since his wife had died, and that his death was inevitable. The children were never shown. Ethan had grown to hate his father, but he still found himself crying at the funeral. Lily was just that bit too young and innocent to understand what had happened, but she cried anyway. A mother dead by cancer, a father by his own hand. They were abused, mistreated, and forgotten, but Ethan and Lily were alive. Although darkness had consumed every crevice of life so far, there were still inklings of hope for them. Their Aunt, who was their mother's sister, took them in. She had one child of her own, who was already an adult and moved out and on.

Time tends to heal all wounds, but it rarely cures the lust for vengeance. Ethan still boiled with anger over the years of battery he suffered by his father's hand. He was more bitter about his inability to implement revenge than he was sad about his dad's death. He wasn't able to hide from it either. As Lily grew older and matured, she began to take on some physical features of their corrupted father. Although she had his chin, dimple, and curled locks, it was the eyes that Ethan couldn't escape from. Each time he caught her eye it was like looking into the eyes that had abused him for 8 years. He couldn't help it, nor did he want it, but resentment for Lily grew within him, simply because of the reminder she paid him daily.

This isn't to say that Ethan ever overtly mistreated Lily. He took care of her, as any older brother would. However, one cannot control subconscious micro-gestures. And so, just as you can tell by means of a 'gut feeling' when someone doesn't like you, Lily felt her brother's distaste for her grow over the years. This led her, as it naturally would, to long for her older brother's approval. All she wanted was for him to appreciate her, but all this desperation did was drive them further apart, as Ethan was further annoyed by her attempts to make up for something that was not in her control, and not even her fault to begin with.

Years moved on. Wounds healed, but Ethan could never move passed hating his dead father. He was an adult now, and Lily would be soon. They weren't as close anymore, but they still kept in contact. After Ethan turned 18, he left his Aunt's house. Lily still lived there. Years of unacknowledged resentment forced an invisible wedge between Ethan and what remained of his family. It wasn't unresolvable, from an unbiased perspective. But Ethan wasn't in an unbiased position, and neither was Lily.

You might say that fate had damned the pair. Their mother, unfairly taken. Their father released them of their torment by taking himself. Lily had always been bubbly and smiley, yet inside there was a sadness. Inside there was a feeling that she was unwanted. Her mother didn't want her enough to fight on. Her father felt death was better than living on for her sake. Her brother distanced himself, and she could never know why. She was sad and lonely and alone. When you're 17 and lost, it's all too easy to fall in with a lost crowd. By the time Lily was 18 she had already been reluctantly introduced to class A drugs, and by 19 she was using frequently.

Overdoses happen. They happen often. They don't always end in death, but they do end that way quite regularly. Lily overdosed on heroin on her 21st birthday. By then she'd been using so often that she couldn't go a day without it. She was an addict. The release drugs offered softened the pain of her past, and the pain of her brother not wanting her. On her birthday, she decided to visit her friend and shoot up there. She didn't even use any more than she usually would, but the change of context and the excitement of the day factored in, and she overdosed at 4 in the afternoon, September 4th, 2018. She was taken to hospital too late, and she died there, shortly after 5 PM, utterly alone.

Ethan woke up on his 26th birthday feeling pretty content. He had a steady job at a nearby insurance agency. Nothing too exciting but the pay was decent. He'd been seeing his girlfriend Sinead for almost 2 years now, and she was expecting. Ethan was happy about that. He hadn't thought about the traumas of his past in quite a while, and even when he did, he was able to deal with the emotions. Sinead had been a huge support to him, and he loved her for it. It was a Thursday, so Ethan had to work. He was chirpier than usual, as everyone is on their birthday, so he didn't mind going to work that day. He left the office at 5:30PM and made the short walk home. As he reached the front door, he felt his phone vibrating obnoxiously in his pocket. He smiled. They hadn't talked in a few months, but he knew it was Lily ringing to wish him a happy birthday.

Ethan always found it strange. He was five years older than Lily, yet they were both born on the same day.

Raindrops & Snowflakes

God is a different thing depending on your perspective. To human ancestors, the Sun was God for a time. To an ant, this is probably still the case. Domestic dogs probably think you, the owner is God. God is subjective, God is an idea or concept. To a raindrop, gravity is God. Gravity is death and life to a raindrop. The same force that brings the raindrop into existence is the one that inevitably closes out the raindrop's life. This isn't to say that every raindrop accepts gravity as God. In many cases, gravity is this evil, immutable force that ends countless lives. But gravity, like the Sun, is pure apathy. A force that cannot care should not care, and Nature finds its way no matter what.

Raindrops spend their entire, brief existence, free-falling as a community. Each droplet, aware of their looming destiny, finds homage in the fact that they shall all perish together. There's a social value attached to group failure. It's a feeling of 'Well at least I'm not the only one'. You can't feel shame or self-loathing when there's no other way for things to turn out. Therefore, each raindrop goes fearlessly into that dark night and stares into the abyss as a community, rather than a group of individuals.

Raindrops are a warm community of beings. As a people, they embrace everyone. They're a resilient, hard-working group. Although the plight of their people is constant, there is no room for self-pity, victimization, or any other behaviour that suggests a belief that life should be fair. Raindrops know that life isn't fair and the embrace it. Although the free fall of their lives ends in unavoidable death, the experience is enjoyed throughout. There is no attempt to panic or attempt to escape. Instead, most raindrops embrace the thrill of the fall. God's spark enlightened consciousness in all particles. Although many forms of this aren't as sentient or as obvious as human consciousness, it still flows through all things. The implicit knowledge of this is expressed in how Nature is commonly referred to as 'her' rather than as a lifeless thing. Just as humans march toward unavoidable mortality, so to do raindrops, just at a much quicker rate, aware of this poetic doom in their own conscious way. Of course, the life of a raindrop begins far before it ever becomes a droplet, but the starting point of consciousness as an actual raindrop is debated frivolously. Some drops believe that raindrop life doesn't begin until the raindrop begins to fall from the clouds, whereas others believe that raindrops are valued as raindrops far before they ever become raindrops, as water condenses and is held as clouds in the atmosphere. There are many examples of such debates in raindrop society.

Let us say, as raindrops do, that any Drop who believes Raindrop life only believes once falling begins is known as a Wet-Drop, and any who believe that Drop live starts before this event is called a Dry-Drop. Both types of Drop had always been important to balance Raindrop society. Each group had its own general beliefs on how Raindrop society should be conducted, and both sides continually compromised in order to create a fair and equal society, to the best of their ability. This balance was built upon the premise that neither side was ever completely correct, and so the humility and awareness of opinion bias was core to the progression of Raindrop society. Raindrop society was an open book which welcomed healthy debate and encouraged the discourse between both Dry and Wet drops. This discourse was key to the progress necessary for raindrops to coincide.

You'll have noticed how all of that was explained in the passive voice. The past tense often implies that once was, is no more. And so this is true too for the Raindrops. The change began with a social climate change. For humans, this manifested as actual climate change. Winters got colder, Summers hotter. However, in the world of Raindrops, the Wet-Drops, in particular, began to become rigid in their held beliefs. They began to believe that there were no valid opinions besides those held by Wet-Drops, and they began to be offended and outraged by any other form of opinion that contrasted their own. They became cold toward their fellow Drops who, for example, believed that Raindrop life began before falling started. The Wet-Drops became cold, rigid and offended by everything that countered their own specific dogma. Then one day the change happened. The Wet-Drops turned into Snowflakes.

Soon enough, snowflakes were everywhere, or at least they seemed to be. Seeing as water expands when it freezes, the Snowflakes were almost twice the size of Raindrops, they were much louder and much more sure of themselves. The Snowflakes made society a much colder place to live in. They froze out any Raindrop that held a dissenting opinion. They became enraged by any Drop, Wet or Dry that even suggested a Snowflake could be in any way wrong After all, each Snowflake was unique and special (Or at least their parents told them that) whereas all Raindrops were identical. The Snowflakes made it so that it was virtually impossible to even remain a Raindrop. Society had grown too cold, and too volatile for Raindrops to thrive. Snowflakes became far more common. A new generation of fragile, self-entitled precipitation. They were blissfully unaware that they were destroying an almost utopian society, by being hypersensitive to any unfavourable facts. Over time, the Snowflakes altered the discourse, so that Raindrops became the unfavourable group within society, and especially Dry-drops, who were most enraged by the Snowflakes.

The problem with Snowflakes doesn't stem simply from their overt disposition to be offended and enraged. It stems from a sub-conscious self-righteous nature. See Snowflakes belie that they are made up of a truer moral fibre. They believe they know better, and so any other voice is dismissed and suffocated because it is not truly morally aware, and so the facts presented by these other voices must be tainted by this lack of morality. What Snowflakes fail to see though, is that Snowflakes and Raindrops are made from the exact same thing; water. Snowflakes only emerge due to an inability to navigate adverse climates. When the going gets tough, so to speak, the water of Wet-Drops hardens, and becomes cold and callous and rigid, and they become Snowflakes. There is still, however, a way for Snowflakes to reverse the ill-advised coldness of their Nature. Simply by leaving some warmth and perspective into their hearts, they can revert back to their Raindrop form.

However, as it stands, it appears that Raindrop society is hurtling towards the extinction of Raindrops completely, only to be left with a society of politically-correct Snowflakes. The climate has become so cold and foreboding, and so discriminatory towards any non-Snowflake, that the only choice is to become a Snowflake. There is no room for Raindrops anymore. There is only room for the dogma of Snowflakes. Humans experience this societal change in Raindrops as climate change or global warming. Still, it is quite possible, or maybe even likely that this was an elaborate metaphor, and if you have become offended in the reading of this description of Raindrop society, then it might be time to check your temperature because you might be a fucking Snowflake.

Epilogue

Business. Confidence. Haircut. Questionable income tax payment. These were just a few of the first words that would pop into your head whenever you saw Peter Brooks. He was the Irish embodiment of Wall Street, sort of. He worked for a small law firm. He drank whiskey; neat. He partook in all the activities that you'd expect of a wealthy, morally questionable white-collar man. He drank excessively. He used cocaine as if the Celtic Tiger had never ended, and he had a different woman for every night of the week. He lived the type of life that every young fella who had never owned a folder in school, dreamt of. He had buckets of cash and very few people within his circle who told him he was living a very temporary type of lifestyle. On top of this, Peter was exceptional at his job, winning case, after case, getting criminals and tax-evaders alike off of years of prison time. He was bad, but he was good.

Peter had built this lifestyle meticulously. He had generated an image, an image that he hoped would outshine any, and all other versions of himself. See, Peter had a dark past. As a young fella in Cork, he'd earned himself a harrowing reputation. He'd undergone minor plastic surgery in an attempt to hide his identity, but some of the older players still knew exactly who he was. He'd been a heavy drinker and a nuisance. He was the guy who pestered pedestrians as they passed on Grand Parade. Asking for money, or just a moment of your time to hear a story. He appeared at nearly every bushing session possible, always noticeably older than anyone else present, and definitely the most drunk. He had a reputation as a pathetic, irritating wino as a young man. What was worse is that he had a brand, a brand he wore with pride at the time, but it was now a reminder of the embarrassment he had become and of the dark path he had taken. Peter had been a lot of things in life, but above all else, Peter was The Sham With The Naggin' Tattoo.

If you enjoyed this book, please consider leaving an online review. The author would appreciate reading your thoughts, and most sales are prompted by reviews from readers like you.

About the Author

Daragh Fleming is a young author from Cork in Ireland. Informed by a background in psychology and linguistics, Daragh's conversational style is complemented by a unique insight into the human condition. This is Daragh's debut collection, which serves as a sign of things to come. Daragh's passion for mental health and the promotion of positive mental well-being is evident in some of the stories in this collection. He uses wit, and detail to create bizarre and enjoyable stories which ensure that the reader comes along for the ride.

Visit his website at https://thoughtstoobig.com

You can also follow Daragh on social media:

Instagram: www.instagram.com/daraghfleming/
Twitter: https://twitter.com/DaraghFleming
FaceBook: www.facebook.com/daraghf3

About the Publisher

Sulis International Press published fine fiction and nonfiction in a variety of genres. For more, visit the website at https://sulisinternational.com

Subscribe to the newsletter at https://sulisinternational.com/subscribe/

Follow on social media
https://www.facebook.com/SulisInternational
https://twitter.com/Sulis_Intl
https://www.pinterest.com/Sulis_Intl/
https://www.instagram.com/sulis_international/

Printed in Poland
by Amazon Fulfillment
Poland Sp. z o.o., Wrocław

55558310R00075